Ceci June

MISSOURI WILLIAMS

The Doloriad

Missouri Williams is a writer and an editor
who lives in London. Her work has appeared
in *The Nation*, *The Baffler*, *The Believer*,
and *Five Dials*. *The Doloriad* is her first book.

The
Doloriad

MISSOURI
WILLIAMS

MCD × FSG Originals | Farrar, Straus and Giroux | New York

The
Doloriad

MCD × FSG Originals
Farrar, Straus and Giroux
120 Broadway, New York 10271

Title-page image by jakubkmita / Shutterstock.com.

Library of Congress Cataloging-in-Publication Data
Names: Williams, Missouri, 1992– author.
Title: The Doloriad / Missouri Williams.
Description: First edition. | New York : MCD × FSG Originals /
    Farrar, Straus and Giroux, 2022.
Identifiers: LCCN 2021044941 | ISBN 9780374605087 (paperback)
Subjects: LCSH: Environmental degradation—Fiction. | Regression
    (Civilization)—Fiction. | Survival—Fiction. | LCGFT:
    Apocalyptic fiction. | Novels.
Classification: LCC PR6123.I55257 D65 2022 | DDC 823/.92—dc23
LC record available at https://lccn.loc.gov/2021044941

Designed by Janet Evans-Scanlon

Our books may be purchased in bulk for promotional,
educational, or business use. Please contact your local
bookseller or the Macmillan Corporate and Premium Sales
Department at 1-800-221-7945, extension 5442, or by
email at MacmillanSpecialMarkets@macmillan.com.

www.fsgoriginals.com • www.fsgbooks.com
Follow us on Twitter, Facebook, and Instagram at @fsgoriginals

10 9 8 7 6 5 4 3 2 1

The theatre director who must himself
create everything from the ground up,
has even first to beget the actors. A visitor
is not admitted; the director has important
work at hand. What is it? He is changing
the diapers of a future actor.

—*Franz Kafka*

The sainthood of the laity is more painful.

—*Clarice Lispector*

The
Doloriad

Prolegomena to Future Agonies

When Dolores inclined her head to acknowledge the presence of her uncle the movement dragged her down toward the earth; her breasts dipped and swung in a low arc and the rest of her droopy, fat body scarcely managed to resist. The wheelbarrow in which the others had placed her wobbled dangerously until their uncle grasped its handles with his trembling hands and began to push Dolores away from the encampment and into the forest. The rest of the children watched them go with little feeling, deadened by light and heat. As she rolled down the slope that led to the green border of trees a great tremor went through her, but Dolores was not able to distinguish between fear and desire and so she made herself still again and awaited her destiny with the wooden resignation of a sinking merchant ship. Her affinity to the earth was so pronounced that she couldn't wait to be in it, though she would never be able to articulate that in words, the trick of which eluded her, and so Dolores had faced up to the marriage and what the schoolmaster called "the dribbling monotony that was promised to her" just as stoically as she'd faced up to being born. She bounced along in her melancholy way, as patient as a stone, and Agathe watched her from the ridge above the path, having followed the two of them at a distance since their departure from the camp. She moved forward, still hidden by the dense net of leaves, and squinted down at the pair in the gully below her. Their uncle shuffled along with his unwieldy burden and the cracked lenses of his glasses repelled the sun; the light bounced away from him, splintering into new delusions, and those bright disks, fixed to the head and the long, dry stick of his body, gave him the appearance of a watchtower on the move. It was no surprise to Agathe that their mother had entrusted their uncle with the transporting of Dolores, the success of which was already a source of much speculation among her children, because his loyalty to the Matriarch was ancient and unquestionable; at all times he bowed to her stronger will. And then there was Dolores herself and whatever soul remained to her after nineteen years of stony submission, although Agathe couldn't find it with her narrowed eyes. The sun slipped through the green canopy above them and moved over her sister's white body. She was a blinding point, all the more blinding given her placement within the bright forest, sodden with light, and suddenly it was painful to look at her. But this was the last sight that Agathe would have of her sister before she was gone with no guarantee that she would ever come back, and so she blinked the tears from her eyes and committed the image to the vault of her memory, scrabbling in the earth with her dirty, restless fingers as if anchoring herself to the damp mulch of the forest floor. The creaking of the wheelbarrow—the whoosh of air as it moved from one side to another, tilting with the weight of her sister's body—her uncle's dry cough. Up on the ledge watching the pair through the screen of vegetation, Agathe felt as though she were really down there, next to her uncle and the wheezing sound he made as he pushed the wheelbarrow along the rough dirt path, and she could smell the sweat pooling in the deep folds beneath Dolores's armpits without having to imagine it. But this sense of herself dispersing, of occupying multiple spaces at once, was something Agathe knew how to dismiss, and so she pushed herself back through the green forest and through the arrow loops of her own dark eyes all the way into her own dark head, and concentrated on the stupid smile she thought she saw on her sister's lips. Even if she had had legs, Dolores wouldn't have known how to use them to get away. There was a poison in her and the theft of her legs had not been enough for it: those melted stumps were simply the sign of that greater corrosion, much as the trappings of a church are only there to point to the presence of the god, and it was this hidden thing, not their uncle, that was leading her into the forest. It was the blunt promise of her anatomy: the slack mouth and the round pig eyes; the antiquated languor of her fat white hands—these small acquiescences all pointed to the answer of a question never asked: a great pale feminine *yes*. Agathe knew all this and knew not to feel sorry for her.

✳ ✳ ✳

"*In primo enim statu sic erat subjectum corpus animae ut nihil in corpore contingere posset quod contra bonum animae foret vel quantum ad esse vel quantum ad operationem,*" the first voice said, and the second voice translated: "In the first age of mankind the body was subject to the soul and nothing could happen in the body that would be contrary to the good of the soul, neither in its being nor in its operations."

There is an ancient agreement between the glass and the light that allows one to pass through the body of the other without hesitation. Today she was the glass and the glass was in her; her head was a great flat plane and the sun slithered through her brain and received no alteration; she was an infinite disk and she could not see where she ended and the whiteness of the void began.

The second voice continued, reading from the page, "Nor does it matter that even then there was a diverse dignity of souls according to the diversity of bodies . . ." and the surface that was Agathe spasmed—something gave in, and she became aware of the world in stages. Before she knew it she was surrounded by the long, light bodies of her siblings and the walls of the sunny schoolroom. She straightened in her seat and looked at her brothers and sisters, who sat in rows with their faces angled toward the light as if they were waiting to receive orders. Propped up in his high chair, the schoolmaster was a black mass silhouetted against the window behind him, gutted of detail, and understood this angling as a mark of his significance, although he was not blind to the glare of absence in their faces. Agathe placed her chin on the hump of her folded wrists and tried to look at him too, but it was impossible to concentrate on anything in this room that had given in so stunningly to the slyness of the forest and the brightness of the sky, and she was not afraid of the schoolmaster and the dark arrow of his attention because it would be equally impossible for him to address any one of them by name, to single them out, and so the schoolmaster never tried, not wanting, perhaps, to shatter either the illusion of his importance or the pretense of the lesson.

He rumbled again, "*Diversa fuisset dignitas animarum, cum oporteat animae ad corpus proportionem esse, ut formae ad materiam, et motoris ad motum,*" and Marta translated laughingly, "A diverse dignity of souls. It is necessary for the soul to be proportioned to the body. As form to matter, as mover to moved . . ." but all Agathe heard was "a diverse dignity of souls." She let her eyes slip out of focus and the line of children in front of her melted into a column, a smooth marble whole. Next she placed her head in her hands and imagined her way into the dead city, gliding through the thinning trees toward the crumbling apartment block where the schoolmaster lived in what used to be known as Vinohrady. It was from this lonely building, half swallowed by the green undergrowth, that the legless old schoolmaster was carried to the school every morning, wrapped up in his habitual cloud of resentment and despair and full of curses and mumbled threats. After wrenching the schoolmaster from his sheets and placing him in the metal wheelbarrow, her brothers would push their portly trophy along corridors where the early-morning light tumbled through defeated ceilings and dark green moss made secret insinuations across the ancient wallpaper, and then down the gentle incline that led from the schoolmaster's apartment to the encampment some three miles distant, Jakub at the handles and Adam guiding the front wheel, while Marek would run ahead and tell the others that they should assemble in what the school-master liked to describe as "that run-down hellhole of a building" because no matter how parodic they believed the process or however meaningless the schoolmaster's lessons, they were preferable, after all, to the other options. Agathe had never seen the city with her eyes, but Jakub had told her about it, and now she followed the thread of his images and saw the weeds pooling in the gaps between the broken tiles, the windows with their shattered panes of glass, and the rotting wooden doors of the apartment blocks, listening all the while to the whispering of the abandoned buildings, which was sometimes mutinous and at other times a lament, and the quiet desolation that shoved and jostled around the bright halo of her brother's hair. When they reached the rotting room where they had their lessons, the schoolmaster droned on about things nobody cared about for as long as he could bear it, and then his pouchy eyes began to droop, fat mouth slackening, and he'd snore and snore until the boys took him home and this was the end of words—there was only the creaking of the wheelbarrow, the rustling of the leaves, and the quiet drip of the dying light through the canopy above them, a great mottling; and so the journey back to the schoolmaster's lair had the cadence of an older dream, a slow, incomprehensible merging. Soon night hailed down upon the old city. The schoolmaster emitted his high snore and fifty feet above him a flock of roosting birds drowsed in the wet wooden rafters of the apartment block, their white droppings mingling with the trickling water from yester-day's rains to form a pale liquid that dripped through the ruined floors and landed on his swaddled form, speckling the blankets and sieving through the wiry mass of his beard . . .

Thunder cracked from somewhere to the north of the encampment and Agathe was dragged back to the schoolroom. She looked around but it was as if none of the others had heard it: the schoolmaster continued to read from the book in front of him, Marta translated, and the children dreamed, staring at the bright window with its sweep of yellow light. The sun slugged through the dirty glass and what emerged on the other side was altered and impure, nothing like the effortless exchange that had earlier absorbed Agathe's full attention, and for a moment this saddened her, bound up as she was in the dribbling time of the room and the encampment beyond it. Outside it began to rain: somewhere near the heart of the forest slow, stupid Dolores would be getting soaked as she waited for the Matriarch's others to come, though none of her siblings were sure that they would. Agathe kicked her legs beneath the desk and leaned down to observe the relative perfection of her own limbs. The hatred she felt for Dolores was thick, indivisible; an indistinct welt of what used to be identifiable moments. She picked away at it anyway, trying to draw out individual images. Dolores sunning her whale-like body in the grass while the chickens scrabbled in the earth around her, the squirming ribbons they dug up premonitioning her own damp fate. The schoolmaster with his round, beady eyes craning over the high edge of the schoolroom window in order to spy her through the tangle of undergrowth, which arranged tantalizing flickers of her legless allure. The boys laughing at her as their uncle wheeled her through the camp, her mouth eternally at crotch level. Agathe dreamed. Not of her own marriage but of Dolores's. She was Dolores as she wobbled her way through the forest, unaware of being watched, the wheelbarrow tilting flirtatiously. Or was it that she was Dolores further back in time? Dolores in the grass with her T-shirt off, the fat brown hillocks of her nipples sticking up in the air. These obscenely resolving themselves into something hard and translucent—the glass; the wet smell of the forest; the drone of the schoolmaster's voice; a diverse dignity of souls.

Agathe slid down from her desk and began to crawl away on all fours. The schoolmaster turned the page and cleared his throat but nobody looked at him. Instead the few children who were still awake watched Agathe as she made for the door. Now the light was dimmer; the clouds blocked out the sun. They had hurried over from the mountains beyond the city and now they hung above the encampment and formed a proximate sky of their own, softer, more forgiving. The afternoon's radiance was quashed. Agathe thought about their mother, and her brain contracted as she tried to come up with an appropriate lie or an excuse for intimacy. Around her the air was heavy with ozone, and the warm rain stirred the earth to thick mud. Jan scurried across the square that lay between the schoolroom and their mother's apartment block, heading for the building on the other side of the encampment that he shared with their older sisters, and she knew that if he saw her hanging around he would put her to work. As she watched him approach, Agathe considered escaping into the empty canteen, or giving up the encampment for the forest, where it would be cool and silent, but she wanted to be near their mother, and so she darted away from the covered entrance of the schoolroom and crawled along the edge of the stone dormitory that bordered the square's lowest side. Jan's eyes were stuck ahead of him and he didn't see her. He rounded the side of the schoolroom and disappeared from sight, and Agathe began to inch in the direction of their mother's quarters. Glowering at them from the top of the sloping square, the apartment block was the tallest building in the encampment, and although the Matriarch never used the upper levels, it was easy enough for Agathe to imagine her spying on them from that commanding height, noting down every one of their errors in a large dusty ledger so that she would never lose sight of who could be trusted and who could not. And this was not so far from the truth, she reminded herself as she scrambled across the muddy square, because her whole life long their mother had had a passion for keeping records, and at night the children would hear her tapping away on the faded keys of her old plastic computer and know that she was thinking of them, though never in the way that they wanted. Agathe clambered up the stone steps at the base of the building and hurried along the short tumbledown corridor that led to their mother's office. The door was open and she stuck her head inside. The Matriarch sat with her arms folded on the wooden desk and her gaze was fixed on the encampment, which she watched through the dirty glass of the window in front of her. She was surrounded by a pool of light that came from a single desk lamp, while her electric wheelchair crouched in the dark corner farthest away from

Agathe. As always, their mother's eyes were hidden by her black wraparound sunglasses and a pale pink quilted shawl covered her broad shoulders. The Matriarch gave no sign that she had seen her daughter approach or heard her footsteps on the peeling linoleum of the corridor outside, and so Agathe studied her face, which was strong and determined and nothing like her own. In the square outside, everything was water, liquid, slipping, blending, but here she was caught in the net of her mother, in the long, narrow jaw with the crooked nose pointing off to one side like a rudder and the thin gray hair spreading out over her iron shoulders in ever-thinner tendrils.

The way it rained in this part of the country was something unique, thought the Matriarch, who was old enough to remember other places and other rains, these memories seeping through the cracked surface of the present, the bright, enameled fiction of the camp, no matter how hard she tried to push them down. As she stared out across the square, the sky pressed in and the world welled up. A flood of tepid water submerged the earth, a little at first, but the rain, like the light, would get stronger. The flood was holy, the Matriarch decided. She closed her eyes and saw a slow sheet of mud and debris roll away from the enclosure of the camp, flowing down the slope and along the former road in the direction of places whose names were sputtering candles in her wet, dripping mind, hissing with ž's, š's, and ř's that she'd been only too glad to forget, and one day the rain would wash them away entirely, the sounds of the dead city and her memories of them, and then the Matriarch would finally be free of it—the past and its language. She sat in her office and the past sloshed around her head, and outside it rained with a fury that belonged to an era remembered only through the hints of the city and the stony belligerence of the abandoned buildings. The Matriarch was coy about this time. She didn't like to think about a time that wasn't bound by her rules, the rituals invented for her family, the order that was uniquely *hers*. She kept her knowledge close to her chest, and their uncle could be trusted not to speak of the time that had preceded their time when the city was full of other people and automobiles of many colors streamed down highways that seemed inexorable as fate. The Matriarch had been born in another time altogether, when the world had been made up of clear lines and definite spaces, and this gave her an advantage over them because as a rule her children were weak, shapeless, and overwhelmed by the enormous lethargy that hung above the empty city and the surrounding forest; if it wasn't for the efforts of the older siblings, Jan and his sisters, the whole lazy lot would perish. The Matriarch had a sense of direction, energy. It had seemed impossible to continue and yet here they were, the Matriarch and her family, and life went on. If she had her way it would never stop. If she had her way it would get bigger and bigger. But the children belonged to this world, not her—"You can tell it from looking at them," their uncle had rasped, sitting in his chair in the dying light, when she'd brought him another one, and there were always more of them, another white baby nestling up against her like a blind, squirming maggot; and who would have ever thought that it would be her to be the one to keep them all alive? The Matriarch opened her eyes and peered through the broken plastic blinds at the muddy disorder of the encampment. The flood was dangerous, she concluded. Although it promised to sweep away the past and its degradations, it, too, belonged to the new world and was part of its leveling, an incessant, deadly mingling. And because the world around them was empty, save for the eyes of the few animals left that watched them from the forest and waited for their end to come too, the flood could only be intended for the Matriarch and her children. The rain hurtled down. She looked up at the sky resentfully.

Agathe knocked on the wooden frame of the doorway. The Matriarch turned to look at her youngest daughter with coldness in her pale eyes and thought about lack. At night Agathe stole away into the woods and often the Matriarch wondered whether her daughter slept at all or whether she simply curled herself up beneath the trees at the place in the forest where their whispering intensified, became a roar, and there retreated—yes, it couldn't really be called *sleep*—into even more soupish patterns of thought. If the others resisted the Matriarch they could be resisted in turn, their rebellions dismantled with words and met with acts whose violence was carefully calculated to exceed whatever provocation had come first. But Agathe, the Matriarch had realized, was different. Her animal body could not be reasoned with, and her daughter could not be brought into line: she was a changeling from the dead city, a stone baby sent to the encampment by a god splitting his sides with laughter to parody the Matriarch and her dreams, a termite in the ark. Agathe said nothing, but her face was a question. What was the Matriarch's dream? Their mother stared into the mirror of her computer screen. She had wanted children, enough children to rebuild the world in her image, and now her daughters sprawled out in the darkness, their brothers lying beside them, a beacon in borderless night. And perhaps if the Matriarch were to creep up on them on one of those indeterminate mornings, she wouldn't be able to tell where one child ended and another began; instead what she would find would be a mass of life, straining at its edges. She straightened up in her chair, disturbed. No matter. Life—it was still life, after all, and the Matriarch had time. The only thing she didn't have time for was doubt. In the weeks before the coming of the rains the Matriarch had at last received a sign, the longed-for message beaming into her willing mind. A lighthouse rotated in the darkness, funneling away at the chaos in its heart, and what emerged was a singular, concentrated light sweeping over the black waters. She saw a family like hers, blond, gray-eyed, living somewhere on the other side of the city, and even if she didn't know how they had reached her, she didn't doubt that they *had* because her whole life the Matriarch had had a certain kind of faith in visions. With the image of a group just like them, and blood, *new* blood, swinging in her mind like an old wooden sign, she had sent away Dolores, poor, fluttering Dolores, to the place in the forest where she knew they would find her. Now the future acquired a new density. One day the city would be full of people who looked like the Matriarch and her brother, and there would be other cities too, her daughters would fill up whole continents. It wasn't over yet! Dolores gone off to be married and the others resting in their beds, a great big lump of life.

The Matriarch didn't move from her seat by the window and nor did Agathe cross the threshold of the door. She looked at her mother and calmly reached for the old lie, repeating the words she had heard the others say in her slow, halting way. "It's time for us to watch the show together. You've forgotten about it, but it's time." The Matriarch didn't believe her. "Then why aren't the others in here bothering me too? Besides, these days you have your own television." Agathe shook her head. "It isn't working, it isn't working . . ." Behind her the encampment was beginning to grow dark, and she was aware of everything in it: the square with its slick of mud, the sagging schoolhouse with the water sluicing through its rooms, the bunched shapes of the dormitory buildings, and there, even farther away, the circle of trees that crowded around the perimeter of the camp; and there was a sense too in which she was still in the forest, watching Dolores trundling along the rough path, as though no time had elapsed since that morning and the day was one impossible simultaneity, the rain churning up not just the earth but the discrete units of human time, although for the most part Agathe followed her own. The chattering of her siblings as they emerged from the schoolroom floated through the open window. In the square in front of the Matriarch's office, Alexandra laughed with her arm around Eva and pulled her toward Jakub, who leaned against the wall of the stone dormitory at the base of the slope with Marta and Mary at his side. Adam sang something without words as he bundled the schoolmaster into the wheelbarrow and began to push him along the path that led out of the encampment, and Marek ran after him. Meanwhile, Franta rolled in the mud like a pig, weak, yellow-toothed, and almost as stupid as Dolores. Agathe watched her brothers and sisters through the dripping window with its film of rain, and it seemed to her that they were no longer her siblings but the heroes from the schoolmaster's old books: bold Marta, swift-footed Jakub, fair-haired Mary, gray-eyed Alexandra, thickheaded Franta . . . A diverse dignity of souls! They mingled in the muddy square, and it was only Agathe who had slipped the schoolmaster's sacred taxonomy, which had only pretended to be encompassing. Soon enough she was overwhelmed by the facts of the present: the cold tiles beneath her feet, the wooden doorframe against her fingers, the pelting of the rain outside. A peal of thunder cracked through the sky, closer now, somewhere to the west of the camp. Her mother was an anchor and Agathe drifted toward her. But time had moved on and the Matriarch's attention had returned to her interminable spreadsheets. She was no longer thinking about the rain, or Agathe, but the practical matters of the camp, the continued survival of their family. She was thinking about a spinning lighthouse. Agathe slid one foot over the threshold of their mother's office. The room was almost as dark as the dimming square outside, night rapidly approaching, and the only clear point was the Matriarch's face in the orange lamplight, which diminished around her in concentric circles. The single crack that chasmed across the computer screen was silvery with interior fire, and on the wall beside the window there was a photograph of the Matriarch and their uncle in a green plastic frame, the image beginning to decay. Beyond the boundary of the circle, a constellation of objects remembered the past, and the screen of the ailing television stood by the side of the far wall, a black rectangle that swallowed the leftover light. The Matriarch turned off her computer and fixed her insect eyes on the mass of papers whispering to one another on the desk. Agathe couldn't remember what she had wanted to say, only that she had intensely wanted to say it, to win something from her mother, anger or praise. She listened to the plaint of the abandoned apartment block that rose up behind her mother, an immense, lonely carapace, and then she tried again. "It's time for the show." The wind scuttled across the square. Someone groaned in one of the dormitories. The television screen was an obsidian promise. Agathe sensed her advantage and pushed on with her speech. "It's time, it's time." The Matriarch ignored her, and so Agathe slithered into the room, crunching her way through the debris toward the television. As she went by, the black glass of the computer monitor reflected her progress; the Matriarch examined the image of her daughter and before she knew it she was thinking about old errors, about the disastrous tangling of their bloodline, and some dark, buried hostility that she could scarcely begin to name.

The sound of Agathe flipping the television switch brought her back to the room—it was this rain, the Matriarch thought, setting everything adrift—and a voice crashed through the silence, a high male voice that spoke in the language of the dead city, which Agathe understood without knowing why. She placed her hands on the cold screen and the familiar music began to play. The title of the show scrolled along the screen in glaring yellow letters, followed by a prancing cartoon sheep. A lone trumpet made itself heard. The voice shouted out the name of the show in heavily accented English—"*GET AQUINAS IN HERE!*" An image flickered onto the screen and Agathe drew back in order to see it clearly. It was a scene from the old world, an ordinary gray room. Two figures sat across from one another at a metal table in a room that looked like an office. Bright pictures were hung at varying intervals on the pale yellow walls and a warm summer afternoon streamed through the only window and lit up the faces of the two women inside. A green potted plant lounged in the corner and a motivational poster that read *If your dreams don't scare you they aren't big enough!* climbed along the wall beside it. Other shadows massed outside the door to the Matriarch's office. "It's time for the show—" They swept inside.

In the television an older woman, probably in her fifties, faced a younger woman, really only a girl, who wore a strange uniform, a red-and-white dress with an image of a dog with a squashed face that grinned and winked at the crowd of children. As their uncle drifted into the Matriarch's office he made his habitual observation that the girl was wearing a cheerleader's uniform, and the siblings nodded without caring, crowding behind Agathe. The older woman was speaking in English, but the Czech voice kept up a mumbling commentary: "*It's that critical moment in any high school movie ... ! The campus is buzzing with suspicion and rumor ... ! Someone has been wronged. Someone's reputation is at stake. Somebody has lost their virginity. And perhaps, in a pamphleteer's wet dream, all three of these statements can be ascribed to the same person ...*" The girl on the screen was shedding large cartoonish tears. The school therapist leaned in and affected a comforting whisper, but she was drowned out by the tinny voice of the Czech commentator. "*Although a whole day has elapsed since the school's last collective sporting event, Shelley is still dressed in her red-and-white cheerleading uniform, the school's logo, a pug with a squashed face, stretched benevolently across the distressed polyester of her heaving bosom . . .*" The camera zoomed in on the worried face of the school therapist before turning back to the cheerleader and examining her properly. Now the siblings could see the bloody metal pole protruding from one trembling shoulder. The commentary started up again in the same bright tone. "*When Shelley shuffles in her wooden chair, metal and bone scrape together in a way that just sounds* so *uncomfortable! Whatever has happened to Shelley? Will she ever cheer again? This brave school therapist is determined to find out.*" As the camera swung back to the school therapist the television went black. Suddenly they saw themselves reflected in the screen, a family in negative, and they didn't like it at all. For a moment they were still and saying nothing, but then the children began to groan. Marta leaned forward and hit the television, and Jan, cursing, shuffled out of the room. Soon Agathe heard the rumble of the backup generator as it lurched into life. She fixed her eyes on the screen.

The school therapist was wary. She eyed Shelley. "Shelley, we can't give you access to medical help until you tell us what happened, who did this to you, and how you feel about it. As school therapist, it's my duty to make sure that your psyche has passed through this ordeal unscathed." She beamed awkwardly. "And you know—having that steel pole bumping against your lungs sure must be uncomfortable!"

Next the school therapist moved a little closer. "Why don't you tell me what happened? Who did this to you? Was it *Brad*?" Marta laughed. Shelley didn't say anything and the school therapist frowned. "We can't help you if you won't tell us what's wrong, Shelley. Anyone can see that you're in pain. But some types of pain are more important than others. I am here to help *you*. And so you have to tell me what happened. I don't like talking to myself, Shelley. We know you like to take risks. We also know that you went to a party at Brad's house and stayed later than all of the other girls. I want you to tell me who did this to you, Shelley, whether it was just Brad or whether there were others, too. I want you to tell me how many *men* . . . You should have listened to your parents, Shelley. They're so worried about you. *We're* so worried about you." Marta adjusted herself in the darkness, and Agathe felt the clammy warmth of her sister's thigh on her skin. She closed her eyes and quietly imagined what it must be like to be Marta and to spend every night with Jakub. When she looked back at the screen the school therapist's face had changed: her friendly, awkward smile had been replaced with a sneer and she narrowed her eyes at the bloodied Shelley, who cringed up against the pole that went through her and continued to cry.

"They told me that you were smart, Shelley. Last year you got some of the highest marks in the school. I'm telling you now that that doesn't matter to people like Brad and the people around Brad who will tear your life into pieces because you let them in once and they know that they can get in again. And I'm not just speaking figuratively. You have to defend yourself. You can't be so weak. What other option do you have? Do you want to say nothing? To see if life can return to normal? It won't. It will get worse. They'll find you, Shelley, and we won't be able to do anything to stop them. We need names. We need facts. You're mistaken if you think those tears can say everything for you. Why are you being so stubborn? They said that you were smart, but I am beginning to see that you are actually quite stupid. And selfish, Shelley. Yes, you heard me. You're selfish because you're not thinking about all the other girls out there who might be suffering in the same way. Do you want Brad and his friends to do this again to someone else? Can you imagine some other girl suffering like you are suffering now? Do you want that on your conscience? I don't think so, Shelley. So *speak*."

Shelley's father threw open the door and it hit the wall with a loud bang and it was clear that he was furious. "I am *so* angry! Who did this to my baby girl?" As he walked into the room the children clapped. The Matriarch rolled her eyes. Drowsing against the concrete wall by the Matriarch's desk, their uncle thought he recognized the male actor from the time before the disaster, or that he had glimpsed that little red face leering at him from a decaying poster or a moldy old photograph buried in a heap of faded magazines. That this second-rate television show had not only enjoyed significant popularity in their own time but had survived the great cataclysm with the same mysterious ease was a continual source of surprise to their uncle, but what he didn't want to remember was that his sister had saved it, hauling a crate of dusty cassettes from the archives buried within the sprawling studio buildings up on Na Hřebenech. She had had her motives, and the less he knew about them the better.

Next to Agathe, Marta squirmed a little, already excited. The school therapist kept her eyes fixed on Shelley. "You need to tell us who did this to you. You're in pain—don't you want the pain to end? Or do you want it to grow, little by little, until something you thought you could manage, perhaps even reduce on your own terms, overcoming it in secret, as a secret, overwhelms you entirely? You won't be fit for ordinary life, Shelley. It will get worse. A little worse, every day. Like *this*." The school therapist stood up from her chair and walked over to Shelley, looking at the weeping girl with a hateful expression before leaning down and grabbing the end of the large metal pole in her chubby hands. "Like *this*, Shelley." She twisted the pole and Shelley screamed and slumped forward. Shelley's father slapped her awake. "Why won't you say anything!" Other characters raced to confront Shelley, a weeping montage of jocks, cheerleaders, friends, and family. Shelley's father grew redder and redder and threw himself at the wall with a desperate wail. Shelley continued to sigh and bleed. Apart from the crackling sound of the speakers—the voice translating the English into Czech, eroding the meaning of what they heard into even more distant dimensions of sense—there was no other sound in their mother's office. They held their breath. Even the Matriarch was caught up in the moment. Eventually, Shelley raised her head and looked at the crowd with small red eyes. She said, "I'll tell you what happened. But only if . . ."

They gasped.

". . . we Get Aquinas in Here!"

They shouted out the tagline at the same time as Shelley; the trumpet roared, the screen went black, and the garish yellow letters of the title scrolled over it again. The room mumbled with approval. Now the problem-solving medie-val saint and his trusty little sheep dashed through their imaginations, fixing the world and pulling the school thera-pist away from Shelley before listening to the cheerleader tell her story with an infinitely patient smile. Marta detached herself from the linoleum next to Agathe and ambled toward Jakub. The Matriarch turned her attention back to her pa-pers and her children ebbed out in a tidal movement. Out-side they organized themselves into pairs and trios before disappearing into the night. But Agathe was left alone in their mother's office. The city was crying. Agathe cried, too, and twisted on the floor. The sunglasses looked down at her, betrayed nothing, and then returned to their work. Lying on the floor with her eyes squeezed shut, Agathe was already miles away from the encampment. Around her the broken facades of the gray buildings were interrupted only by the strange, trembling columns of vegetation that had reclaimed the dolorous city, and these were afraid too. Her cries were echoed through the interminable corridors of empty apart-ment blocks with black, abyssal windows, and something stirred and sighed in the grave of the city center. But there were no rats; everything was dead for miles, save for the old schoolmaster, and now Agathe drifted into his dilapidated building on the edge of Vinohrady. The schoolmaster opened his eyes, looked up at the ceiling, and felt a deep sense of unease despite his swaddling and the fabled secu-rity of his nest. He was thinking about the city. He wanted to forget that the city existed, to extricate himself once and for all from this tangle of metal and stone and forsake it for the softer, more welcoming landscape of his dreams, but he couldn't. If he were to have his way his slumber would never be interrupted. He would stay, nestled underneath the moth-eaten wool of his blankets, a great moth himself, and dream for another eternity. The sun couldn't touch him in here, though he knew that it peeled through the holes in the ceiling high above him, the terrible whiteness of this new age scarring hieroglyphs, secret codes, and hidden threats into the moldering wallpaper of the upper rooms. But it couldn't get him in here, buried beneath his heap of blankets like a great, fat baby. And yet the children always came for him, hauling him out of his bed and carrying him to a building far away where he repeated the impulses of his memory until the night fell again and they took him back to his lair. He couldn't get away from them. The children and their drooling faces wove themselves into his dreams, listening, always, to something that he couldn't hear—to the forest, perhaps, or the poison that wended its way through their thin, choking veins. Or maybe they listened to some vast transmitter tower from the old world, something that hadn't switched off with everything else, and as they listened it insinuated things about him, their mother, and their uncle and told them to wait for a change that was inevitable, one that couldn't be postponed forever. Something that the adults didn't know about because they couldn't hear the tower, or if they could, understood it only as a dim buzzing somewhere at the edges of a used, dried-up scab of a mind. And they would be caught with their trousers down, unprepared! The

schoolmaster could see the transmitter tower in the black-
ness behind his eyelids as clearly as though he himself had
been there in another life, and it was a huge construct of rust
and steel that reached into the sky like an insolent needle.
The air around it was static with expectation and barely re-
pressed power, a soupy thickness in which thunderclouds
gathered obligingly. The children vibrated and looked out
the window. What was it that they were always looking at?
And who was in charge of this imaginary tower? What did
they want from him? It was the ritual, the dividing up of
time, Jakub had implied as much to him once, during one of
their habitual carting-alongs, his golden hair flashing in the
too-bright light. Time, time was the problem. Their time
changed from the time that he had known. Himself nestled
up like a great black moth in the scratchy, moth-eaten chrys-
alis of his bedding, aging, changing too. How long had he
been here? Idiots. His legs were gone. That was why they
had to carry him. But the schoolmaster couldn't remember
where they had gone or who had taken them. Had he lost
them in the first movements, during any of the skirmishes
that had preluded the war? Or had they disappeared in the
cataclysm, when the cold fire of eternity had separated the
wheat from the chaff? Or even later—was it the light that
had eaten them, piece by piece, the hard, bright light that was
looking for him even now, that had taken their minds too?
He couldn't answer these questions. If the light were to
come in, if the ceiling were to fall in completely—he wouldn't
be able to get away. He would have to withdraw into his
woolen shell and wait for the children, but the schoolmaster

couldn't say with certainty whether they would move him to safety or not, because it was a possibility that they would simply watch him burn and the last thing that he'd see would be those gap-toothed, drooling smiles.

In his darker moments the schoolmaster wondered if he would ever be free. The children invaded his life day in and day out, the sanctuary of his quarters interrupted at intervals by their blathering, the unwelcome trips to the schoolroom, and the relentless intrusion of the light. Sometimes the Matriarch asked him questions about them. She would motor up to him in her electric wheelchair as they carried him through the rotting wooden doorway of the schoolroom—which, he remembered now, was not just "a building far away," but the old hematology department at the FNKV on the edge of Vršovice—and as if obeying some silent signal from their mother the brats would lean him against the dirty wall and that witch would have her interview with him. He would shiver then, a limbless egg inside his faded red flannel dressing gown, and try to collect the looseness of his thought into a single thread because everything about that bitch was sharp and murderous. How unbearable it was to look at her, sitting in the electric wheelchair like a mad old queen, the haggard face with its gaunt cheeks arcing in subtle mimicry of the cheap plastic line of her wraparound sunglasses, the acne-pocked texture of her skin, and her short, fat fingers! She would ask him questions about her children: how they were doing, what they were learning, if they paid attention to him, and underneath it all was another question, the one she couldn't stand to ask, which was whether the light had gotten at them too. Naturally she knew the answer. How could she not, spying as she did from that window at the top of the slope, surrounded by her spreadsheets? It was the ritual, the dividing up of time; or it was simply that she wanted to torment him with her presence. The schoolmaster hid his feelings. He answered her in the terse, fluttery voice that belonged to his head and told her nothing of note. But sometimes he spoke about their spirituality, their connection with one another, the beauty of their fraternal relationships. And in his sly voice there were the glances they exchanged with one another, brother to sister and back again, and the mutual disappearing that happened in the breaks between lessons; the slow thumping of movements dimly heard and the moans of pleasure that floated from the edge of the forest back to the classroom. The schoolmaster gloazed over these things, but he knew that his hints were understood; that his arrows found purchase somewhere in the space behind the impenetrable plastic of her lenses. He couldn't remember the color of her eyes. He couldn't remember if she'd had them. The coupling, the denaturing, the unnaturalness of the camp—if only some god would appear and sweep them all away; if only it could rain and never stop raining and carry "this last bastion of humanity" over the edge and into the void. The schoolmaster was tired. He dreamed of a flood. Agathe could see the black water crashing through his head. She wanted to climb into his woolen cocoon too and bury herself deep within those dusty layers, perhaps even feel the illicit heat of his flattened body, but she could feel herself back at the encampment; the cold grittiness of her mother's floor. *Back—come back now*, it sang to her, and the tiny stones welcomed her too.

* * *

A white hand against black wood. The wet smell of the dew on the grass. Morning's chill ghosting over her pale, mountainous shoulders. Dolores shuffled in her skin as though she wanted to shuck it off, and the hand that she had placed on the wooden gate of the encampment trembled. The others were all asleep. She lifted her big cow eyes to the sky and stared at the remainder of the moon, limned with heliotrope. Next she looked over her shoulder at the wet reproach of the forest through whose depths she had so recently struggled. Her dress was translucent, heavy with water, muddied and ragged. The forest whispered: *Come back*. Dolores shook her slow head two times. It was cold outside, and she wanted to crawl into the bed that she shared with her siblings. The pale, bulbous onion of her palm, speckled with black dirt. Her clear body delineated by pink light. The dark wall of trees behind her. Morning's chill ghosting over her pale, mountainous shoulders. And what else? Ah yes—the purpose. She wanted to crawl into the bed that she shared with her siblings, but she had been gone for so long that she had forgotten where they were, which bed was hers, and whose naked arm it was that she used as a pillow. The camp was before her, only Dolores was not certain where she belonged. She was not sensitive to the passage of time; all she understood was that she had left in the wheelbarrow with her uncle and then she had crawled back again without him. Dragging her large, wet body through the thick mulch of the forest floor, moving slowly, arm following arm, hunger tarring her insides—and what had she eaten?—these sensations lingered in her mind as physical memories untrammeled by time; a single and indivisible experience of being. Without the dull repetition of their day-to-day routine her memories of the camp had slid away from her, leaving only the blurry faces of her siblings, her mother, and, of course—*longing*, the tugging and pulling of her corrupted blood. Dolores leaned against the damp black wood of the gate and stared into the encampment as if she were seeing it for the first time. Dilapidated buildings rose to meet her gaze, arching their backs like great stone cats in the first weak sun of the day. An apartment block with a battered head keened in the distance and she realized suddenly that her mother lived there, her quarters spread out across the first floor. The smaller buildings leaned into the larger, clumping around the base of this abbreviated tower, and the ground below was dotted with fallen debris, the apartment block incessantly hounded by the wind that blew in through the forest. Her siblings slept in the low gray faculty buildings. But where should she go? A new image swam into her mind: Narrow eyes and dark hair. Elbows digging at her. Agathe. She should avoid Agathe. The light grew. Dolores lowered herself back down into a crawling position and dug her fingers into the earth and began to pull herself forward. She had a vague feeling that she didn't want to be seen, especially by their uncle—but *why*?—and so she didn't crawl to the center of the camp, the sloping square before the apartment block, but instead headed to the edge of one of the outer buildings, the stone rectangle that was nearest to her, thinking that she could wait there for some other to emerge, because the presence of one of her siblings might give her a clue, a hint as to where her place might be. Her soft belly slid across the wet dirt and her dress was ridged by the mud and the movement into wide limpid folds, so that Dolores resembled nothing more than a huge pupa with her cocoon trailing behind her, wriggling toward safety. She realized that she was wriggling away from something that had terrified her, that it was for this reason she had crossed the wide expanse of the forest at night, scrabbling through the dark undergrowth—her uncle had taken her away, that was why she didn't want to see him—and making her way back to the place of her birth with the inevitability of a homing pigeon. But where had she been? What was it that had scared her? Dolores remembered a man, or thought she did. She groped for an image unsuccessfully. There was almost nothing in her head. After Dolores reached the security of the building, she pulled herself upright again. What else? The sound of water, a building made of white stone, a net of green leaves. She closed her eyes and tried to think about the man, how her mother had described him. Where had he gone? There was a pain in her ribs. Perhaps he had kicked her, as the others so often did. Perhaps he had kicked her and she had crawled away into the forest. Was it as simple as that? Her uncle would know. He might take her back. He might take pity on her. Or perhaps he would know that the man and the kick were a ruse and that all Dolores had seen was the unspeakable green forest and all she had felt was loneliness,

true loneliness, for the first time in her short life. He had left
her there. He had taken her away from her siblings. No—she
wasn't sure of anything. Inside Dolores's skull her uncle rat-
tled about and reached no conclusions. She waited by the
wall, stricken with thought. A giggle floated out from the
window above her. It was the voice of one of her sisters: Was
it Marta? Or Mary? Or another sister altogether, an even
older sister, one of the many whose names she could never
keep in her memory? As she listened, the giggle turned into
a moan that reminded Dolores of school days spent sunning
herself at the edge of the forest while her head exploded into
nothingness, the sounds she heard coming from the vegetation into which her siblings disappeared in twos and threes.
They never asked her to come with them. She felt the cockroach eyes of the schoolmaster crawling over her skin from
time to time, but he never approached her and instead she
curled up in the grass and waited without hope that her
waiting would end: a pale, lonely sphere; an igloo in the
scorching light. Moaning, thumping. Her hot face against
the cool stone. The others squirming in their beds. The cry
her sister made as she fell backward onto the mattress. Dolores looked up at the sky and noticed that the moon had
disappeared. The sun was rising; the light hit the brown
trunks of the trees and shattered across their irregular surfaces. She could sense motion—the clockwork mechanism
of the camp swung into play. All around her people were
stirring. Soon someone would come out of one of the rectangular buildings and see Dolores: Would they help her? Or
give her food? Or would they know without asking that she
had crawled away from her husband? Her fingers were red

and raw, the wide bones of her shoulders aching with effort. She feverishly longed for her mother's embrace. Dolores inched along the stone wall until she reached the corner of the building, and then she pivoted herself around it and continued to inch toward the next corner, where she would be able to see the entrance to the Matriarch's apartment block. Her siblings were waking up. She could hear their high, screechy voices, their laughter, and the building to which she clung was filled with the sound of activity. The swinging of the wooden gate behind her let her know that her brothers had left for the old schoolmaster, although she'd been so occupied with her inching that she hadn't heard them pass. When Dolores reached the edge of the building she was able to narrowly glimpse the corner of her mother's apartment block, framed by the gray concrete lines of her own building and the derelict ward on an angle just opposite. She would tell her mother how it had been: black eyes, watching her from above; she had crawled away; he had done nothing to stop her. She would ask her mother for help. But could her mother be relied upon to give her help? The sun winked down at Dolores and the dark green heads of the trees peered over the wall that surrounded the encampment. The forest said: Come back.

Dolores watched their mother's building for any sign of life, and soon enough she lost herself in waiting; when Agathe tumbled out from beneath the concrete overhang as if someone had given her a shove, Dolores wriggled all over with surprise. Her younger sister picked herself up off the ground and looked around. A moment later Jakub emerged from the shadows behind her. Dolores hugged the wall as closely as she could. They couldn't see her. They weren't looking for her. There was no reason why her siblings should seek her out, save for the old desire to pain and be pained, but as far as they knew she was miles away from the camp, had passed into another realm entirely, a land peopled with suggestions. Had she left their minds already, her memory flowed away? Dolores scrunched up her face. Yes—if the encampment were a smooth-surfaced pond it would not register the removal of a certain unit of water nor retain the shape of its absence; the essential form would remain unchanged. And just as Dolores could not preserve their names and faces in the primer of her mind, so too would her siblings give her up, although she had always taken their recognition for granted. She shook her head sadly and placed her hands on the swell of her empty belly; a low and silent wail welled up in her soul. But Agathe heard it anyway and found Dolores with her searching eyes. So Dolores had returned to the camp! She stared at her sister, where she cowered behind the corner of the dormitory building on the other side of the square, understanding without effort that Dolores was hiding because she didn't want to be seen by her and Jakub. Doubtless she had wanted to reach the Matriarch without encountering any of the others because these encounters would confuse her, derail her from her purpose. This conserving of energy or intent was essential to the life of the encampment, which, despite their mother's best efforts, was plagued by an unholy lethargy, a continual slackening of the will. The Matriarch laid down the law, or what their uncle would describe as a simulacrum of it, and intentions like barricades sprang up around the citadel of her body. On

their mother's orders the children combed through the ruined suburbs for supplies and filled the encampment with
their own children, and she watched them through the dirty
glass of her office window. Nevertheless, it was impossible
to tell whether their hearts were in it, the extent to which
they shared her vision, and the Matriarch wasn't sure which
idea tormented her more, the idea that she forced them to go
against their natures or the idea that they liked it, that the
drive she saw in them toward procreation was not hers but
theirs, a mania for begetting that did not depend on their
mother and her image of the future. Despite the exhaustive
nature of her records, the children remained a mystery to her,
just as she was to them. It was rare that the Matriarch allowed
them to see anything of herself—she dominated their world
but had little to do with it. Was this behind its failure to live
up to her sense of what it could be? Though Jan did his best
to drag an effort out of them, the younger siblings fell prey
to the same monstrous carelessness that had haunted their
eldest brother from the day of his first rousing into duty, in-
ertia written into their bones with letters faint and imperceptible, as though the hand that scrawled them didn't much
care either. Dolores, with her slack white stupidity, was his
number one enemy.

Now Agathe nudged Jakub and pointed at the protruding mass of their sister. He caught sight of Dolores and
laughed, the sound echoing across the empty square and the
slow, unstoppable awakening of the forest around them.
When Agathe looked at him again Jakub was smiling. "She's
back! She's left her imaginary husband all alone in the forest." A shadow dashed over his face. Agathe swung back to

Dolores. The enormous curve of their sister's rear end easily surpassed the gray line of the wall, along with one pale shoulder and a straggle of blond hair; the sodden folds of her dress pulsed with expectation. Agathe repeated Jakub's words to herself: "She's left her *imaginary* husband," and it seemed to her that they burned with a strange fire. "We can see you, stupid!" The folds trembled; a big, timid face leaned into view and waited, but the apartment block was silent and there was no help to be had. Jakub guessed what Dolores was thinking and gestured to its desolate windows. "She's probably already seen you. But she'll be angry, Dolores, because she didn't expect to see you again. They left you in the forest for a reason, and you've disobeyed her, you've spat all over that reason, you've *ruined her plan*—" Dolores's mouth was a black circle of despair. "And so now she's getting ready to mow you down in her big red chair. She's climbing into it right now and pressing that little lever and the chair is beginning to move—remember how it *slides*, it doesn't even make a sound—and she's thinking about how naughty you are, Dolores. She's wondering why you've left your nice new husband, because you've always been so *good*—and now she's gliding toward you and she's *angry*, Dolores, angrier than you've ever seen her—" Agathe joined in with a high, practiced imitation of their mother's voice. "I didn't expect it from you—to be so *ungrateful*—all of you children, such *ungrateful*—" and then Marta leaned out from the dormitory window that looked onto the square and screeched, "—so *ungrateful*, it's *disgusting* how you are—" Dolores dropped back down to the wet earth and began to crawl in the direction of the schoolroom, bellowing with fear. Agathe and Jakub collapsed too, twisting with laughter. Marta placed her elbows on the rusty white metal of the window frame and watched Dolores crawl away with contempt in her gray eyes. Jakub grabbed Agathe's arm and tugged her down the slope. By the time they reached Marta, Dolores was hurtling down the muddy path between the schoolroom and the long building that housed their canteen. "She wasn't supposed to come back," Marta said, rubbing her eyes, and Jakub responded in a singsong voice that made Agathe think he was not only laughing at them but at the encampment and everything in it, "Maybe the others weren't so nice to her." They watched Dolores disappear in the direction of Jan's quarters. "No one is ever nice to her," Marta replied. Agathe, slumping against the dormitory wall, began to smile again. Above them the white clouds were beginning to disperse, a bright blue sky on the edge of emerging. Marta went on, "That's why the Matriarch sent her away. She didn't want to risk anyone else, not even you, Agathe." Agathe jabbed at the earth with a stone and said nothing. Jakub looked at Marta. "But there aren't any others. Did you really think that there were others? Nobody has ever seen them. She's gone mad. She had a *dream*." He glanced back at the apartment block. "She sent Dolores away to die in the forest. Our uncle took her as far as he could. It's a miracle she crawled back." Marta stuck out her tongue. "There are others. Jan told me. The others are just like us, but they live on the other side of the city, in the middle of the forest. Near Beroun—that's what he said." Jakub scowled. "Jan has never been farther than the Vltava—how would he know what's on the other side of the city? He's looked at a map, that's all, and you're impressed because he knows how to read off a name." Now Marta was irritated. "He's older than you. He knows more than you do. I want there to be others too. I want to have children. That means swapping."—"Things don't exist just because you want them to."—"They do! They do!"

The two of them continued to quarrel and Agathe looked up at their mother's building. That morning she had canted into one of those strange, lopping dreams that stank of metal and fire, and although she had been aware of her body windmilling on the bed, for once there had been no pain, only the same sunny surrender she had felt in the schoolroom, as though she were all surface, rising up with nothing beneath her and the world all straw . . . Agathe had woken in the covered area between the apartment block and the partially demolished building beside it to Jakub leaning over her. In the aftermath of these dreams it was his habit to dog her with questions, though she was never able to respond in the way he wanted, in the ordered sentences that her older siblings were able to produce, managing instead only a few scattered words delivered in the senseless speech of the younger children, no real memories at all. But these interrogations were all she had; she craved his attention but didn't know how to encourage it, being so much younger than the sisters in which he was truly interested and unable to marshal her fainting, gasping thoughts into a coherent line. At times they had tortured Jan's children together, but this mutual cruelty did not make Agathe happy, far from it, because she knew that she was closer in kind to those children, with their blurred features and soft skulls, than she was to the long-limbed certainty of Jakub and her siblings, and so as she watched Jakub bully and harass their nieces and nephews she was never unconscious of the fact that she was simply laying down the foundations for a later brutality, next time aimed at her. As her siblings argued beside her she thought about the Matriarch, whose ideas moved along the careful channels she had carved out for them, and which were the opposite of her own, because even when she was in their world Agathe was flickering, unstable, and found it hard to collect her thoughts. She was aware of the disordered nature of her mind, the connectedness of substances, the extreme similitude of objects, the thin boundaries between times and places, so easy to get lost between, and she remembered the phrases their uncle had whispered when she'd told him those things: *associative loosening, cognitive drift.* It was the light that dizzied her, or the smell of the trees at night; these things unraveled her, and whatever was left was free to go places that the others could not because they were single points on the map, but she, Agathe, was the map herself. Even their mother took an interest in the shattered images that Agathe carried over from her dreams, though she was, too, disgusted by those weak, flailing movements. How was it, then, that the Matriarch had had a vision? Agathe tried to picture that legendary control loosening, but she couldn't.

The sun hauled itself over the apartment block and now Marta and Jakub were really shouting at one another. When Agathe looked at the building's entrance again, the Matriarch was watching them, sat in her red electric wheelchair on the crumbling stone platform that lay before her office. Her black sunglasses reflected the pale disk of the sun, one on each lens, and these two circles reminded Agathe of the question of their mother's eyes, whether she'd ever seen them, or whether the lenses were simply part of her, the dark plastic burrowing through her white skin and over time welding itself to the ridges of her cheekbones. The Matriarch watched them with her slow, predatory gaze and Agathe knew that they should join the others, head for the schoolroom, and leave Dolores to her fate—it was already light!—but Jakub had seen their mother too. He reached forward and put his hand on Agathe's head, grabbing her hair and pulling it so that she was forced to look at him. Marta slid away from the window, back into the dark dormitory where their siblings were all beginning to wake up, and Jakub said to Agathe, "She sent Dolores away and one day she'll send you away as well." Agathe replied, "I don't want to go away," and Jakub gave her hair a jerk that brought tears to her eyes; her small white face crumpled into a grimace. She could hear Jan's voice in the distance, bossing the others around, but she couldn't remember who he was or what he wanted because the sharp pain from her scalp and her proximity to Jakub interfered with her connection—always tenuous— to the present; her thoughts rushed away from her. The Matriarch was a bird, one of the few birds left; the sun honed in on Agathe.

* * *

Nothing violent is eternal, he thought, and looked at his sister. Another thing came to their uncle then and it was this: *To question the perfection of the creatures is to question the perfec-*

tion of the power that made them. He couldn't remember where it was from or who had said it but the powerful truth of this claim reverberated through his frail body. Outside his sister's office the encampment was creaking to life, and again their uncle was overwhelmed by the idea that intruded on his mind in regular intervals. The imperfection all around him—it was true that the Creator was gone. As usual this conclusion cut through the hebetude of his daily existence, the thread of which was woven into the dull warp of their collective enterprise, "the sole brightness in the void"— though it could hardly be understood in those terms, being so purposeless, so ugly—and he became aware of a relentless sadness somewhere beneath the surface of his soul, slopping around in the pitted basin of his stomach, and he turned his face away from the Matriarch in order to hide his sudden pain from her eyes that missed nothing. The necessity of this perpetual forgetting, the hiding of the past beneath the successive layers of the unchanging present, drained him, though the light that burned away memory and desire helped too, helped him forget his memories of the old world in service of hers, the faint hope that humanity could live on slowly dying within him when he looked into the empty eyes of every wailing infant that emerged from his sister's uterus. In the nights when he was able to avoid her company, he was bold enough to think about the university, and the same agony overcame him. The abandoned citadels of his dreams; an old library in the mountains through whose limitless corridors he was sure he'd once walked— where had these things gone? The fire that had purified the earth had taken them too, though there had been no evil in them, only beauty; and although his sister maintained that the disaster had been a purge, their uncle could not be so certain when faced with the pitiful mess of the survivors, who—it could not be argued otherwise—lived in a kind of torpid sin, a lethargy and lust that corroded any claim to a higher moral purpose, the necessity of survival, or the particular worthiness of their species, and so over time he had come to see them as simply forgotten. The departed gods had left their task incomplete; they had neglected to wipe away these last remnants of their great error, and in the vacuum of their intention these things had *bred* and clung on to a meager existence in a world more inhospitable than ever simply because "nature hateth emptiness." And meanwhile the city loomed behind them like a great stone disgrace, and the silent forest slunk into their dreams and rooted away at their minds. The few birds that passed this way died quickly, and the boys would bring their corpses home without wondering why they had died because phenomena like this arose from the secret laws of the new world, the only world they had ever known, and which consequently they considered unchanging, as immutable as their uncle had believed the world from which he himself had come. When they ate the birds they were sick but did not die, and their uncle wondered whether this, too, was proof of his sister's defeat, as if born in the aftermath of the cataclysm, the children had been tainted so absolutely that a subsequent poisoning could make no difference. Looking at them on those bright, hopeless mornings, their uncle saw nothing but a copse of stunted trees that were nevertheless suited to their environment in a way that he was not, because though they shared his blood the children were not like him or their mother, and the language they spoke when they were alone together, sure of being unwatched, was neither the language of the city nor the English that he spoke with his sister; the nouns, it was true, were from the city—from their *aunt*, he thought, and the pain came back again—he heard them say *voda, tma, ptáček*, but the way that the words hung together to produce meaning had a logic that he could not follow, and sometimes he thought that this was because they spoke in images, immediate, sensuous images, that their minds had escaped the temporal relationships that had defined the language of the past and instead they lived in an eternal, causeless present, a world of pure simultaneity. There were still animals, after all, the frogs croaking on the edge of the forest, the crickets whirring away at night, and Jakub had sworn that he had seen a *rat* somewhere in the middle of Žižkov—but this couldn't be true! There were no other mammals that close to the city center, except for the schoolmaster—and the children were closer to those animals who thought in sensations and simple images, that was all. With exceptions, of course. There were Jakub, Jan, some of the others. And they thought; they schemed. His own thoughts were so confused these days. If nothing violent was eternal, then why had they persisted on this muddy globe?

His sister yawned. The first light of the day trickled over her old skin, but she wasn't looking at him any longer; instead she stared out the window at Jakub and Agathe, who were playing on the damp stretch of land just before the apartment block. A moment later she climbed into the electric wheelchair and slid down the corridor into the light, and he was alone again. Their uncle shambled over to her desk and wiped the dirty window with his dirty sleeve. Outside, Jakub had his hand in his sister's hair and he was pulling it so that Agathe contorted with pain, and although their uncle could not see his face clearly he was sure that Jakub was smiling. The untangling of sibling relationships was impossible, allegiances in the encampment shifting quickly and unpredictably, but their uncle tried it anyway and his forehead crinkled with effort. Had Jakub taken an interest in Agathe? But none of the siblings had time for their youngest sister, who was only ever halfway in their world. After Jakub released his grip on his sister's hair, Agathe fell to the ground and began to shake with those uncontrollable movements that marked the onset of her visions (or *seizures*, their uncle whispered to himself when he knew no one was listening, subverting, however privately, his sister's narrative) and Jakub looked down at her with an unreadable expression before turning away, exiting the scene via one of the narrow pathways between the stone rectangular buildings that housed the Matriarch's infinite brood; "Their hope for the future," their uncle hissed quietly. Agathe quivered in the dirt.

If Only Someone Would Get Aquinas in *Here* (i)

The schoolmaster leaned over, a puff of black robes, and read to them from the dusty book on the desk in front of him. Today the world was weaker: a milky sun hung in the sky and wanted nothing to do with the earth. What seeped through the cracked glass of the window behind him was a thin, soupy light that washed the schoolroom a bleached yellow, and this meant that the schoolmaster was more visible than ever—a short, fat figure sat in a plastic high chair originally intended for small children, no brilliance to hide him. He lifted his big head from the book and looked out across the room. Before him the aisles of children dipped and dreamed like minnows in a stream of bright water. The younger ones—Jan's children—tried to remain upright, rocking back and forth as they struggled with a sleep that came in waves, and they did so because they were afraid of the schoolmaster and his mumbled threats, whereas the older siblings had no fear and therefore no longer feigned attention. Adam slumped across the wooden desk in front of him, fast asleep, and Jakub rested his head on his brother's tanned shoulder, his face tilted toward the schoolmaster and the warm glare of the window and his eyes half-closed. Franta snored with his body thrown back in his chair, his open mouth and long nose pointed up at the ceiling, while Marek was nowhere to be seen. But it was the girls who were the worst, the schoolmaster had observed on numerous occasions, because they were as stupid as cows and had no respect at all for either him or his lessons. Dolores reclined on the floor beneath her desk, dressed today in a stained cotton shift with a faded logo on the front, stretched beyond deciphering across the bulwark of her breasts. She giggled to herself and didn't even glance toward the front of the classroom and the lectern from behind which the schoolmaster regarded them coldly. In the middle of the schoolroom, Marta and Mary whispered to one another in their filthy language, while two seats away from them Eva buried her head in the cradle of her arms. Alexandra's eyes were also shut and the light climbed up her round cheeks and painted them amber. At the very back of the classroom Agathe rocked in her chair with one small finger inserted into her nose. The schoolmaster moved forward, deeper into the book. "'Thereafter, would that I were not among the men of the fifth generation, but either had died before or been born afterwards. For now truly is a race of iron, and men never rest from labor and sorrow by day, and from perishing by night; and the gods shall lay sore trouble upon them.'"

The wind picked up as he spoke and a scurry of dead leaves and mosses skipped over the concrete floor in front of Agathe, having entered through one of the many holes in the outer wall. Around her the schoolroom was creaking like a ship. She looked at the ceiling, where ivy climbed along the rafters and hung in a thick cloud, here and there shot through with the shafts of yellow light formed by the holes in the sagging metal roof. The walls that closed them in were black with damp, and the contents of the few bookshelves were sharp with blue and orange mold. Beneath Agathe's bare feet, green, gray, and ocher mosses slunk up through the broken floor, blossoming flatly across the crumbling surface of the concrete. She kicked her legs out and thought to herself that the schoolroom was as besieged as one of the schoolmaster's storied cities, the forest invading on all sides. Even Jan's chickens liked to roost here at night, and behind the schoolmaster the surface of the tall blackboard was speckled with bird droppings. In the children's memory this board had never been used; the schoolmaster did not move from his high seat and nor did he summon any of them to the front of the classroom. This was part of the pact that had sprung up between them; a web of quiet agreements that delineated the boundaries of the possible, dictated what could and could not be expected of them. And if a child were to be summoned to him and were actually to come, a piece of chalk pressed into its sweaty little hand, then the fantasy of the schoolroom would be stretched to its edges—because of course almost none of the children could *write*—and nobody wanted that. As they were neither summoned nor commanded, the imaginary scratchings of this hypothetical child threatened no one, least of all their mutual fiction, the game of their learning, and so the rigmarole of education continued, saving them from other types and qualities of time.

Although the schoolmaster kept on moving his lips, the

light was stronger now and ate up his words before the children could hear them. What were the gods to them anyway, living, as they did, in a time that he said was beyond all other times? Outside the clouds rolled away to reveal the sun. A river of light rushed into the schoolroom through the frontal window and turned the black robes of the schoolmaster into an inky shroud, his face a dark field, robbing him of detail and texture. And soon he would feel the warm fingers of the light on his chubby nape and the heat would creep into him, and the dreams, too—he'd lose his thread; the printed matter before him would tram up its meaning, and the schoolmaster would think for a moment that he could hear it, the sound that he believed they listened to, nothing like the scholastic stupor of the schoolroom but an agile and effortless whirring, something that reminded him of machinery, a clockwork teleology, brimming with intent, and then he'd close his eyes and leave his body and trace it all the way back to its origin: the radio mast buried deep in the forest, glinting red and white metal against the dark green of the surrounding trees and heavy with bright umber rust. But Agathe didn't know about any towers. She sighed and brushed his thoughts from her mind. In a few minutes the schoolmaster would be asleep; his big, doggy head would drop down into the yellowing pages and he would drowse until the bell rang for food and work, but now he tried again. "'There will be no help against evil,'" the schoolmaster said, narrowing his eyes at the nearest child. "'Envy, foul-mouthed, delighting in evil, with scowling face, will go along with wretched men one and all. And then Aidôs and Nemesis, with their sweet forms wrapped in white robes, will go from the wide-pathed earth and forsake mankind to join the company of the deathless gods: and bitter sorrows will be left for mortal men, and there will be no help against evil.'" Their eyes were shut, screwed up against the light and him. He could feel it burning into the back of his head. The black weight of his robes. The heavy air of the schoolroom. Time slowed down; a terrible weariness came over him. He felt his eyelids beginning to droop. But the book stared up at him with contempt in its paper face. The schoolmaster harrumphed to himself: What did the book know? It was a snarl of dirty old words, a mess of theological scruples. Yes, it was bound up in the questions of the past, in riddles and contradictions that were never solved because no one cared to solve them; the book belonged to a forgotten world, and so what possible significance could it have for the children in front of him? He'd given up words like *good* and *evil* and *hell* for drowned. And besides, the book was dead. Apocrypha! He marshaled himself, straightened up in his swaddling. When did the world become so full of things?—the living fact of the light; the trees that whispered among themselves; the black eyes of the apartment block; the sad stone city; and a book that stared right back at him. The book was dead and contained only dead things, yet it seemed to him that it burned with a life that didn't belong to it and it was this that he felt when he brushed his fingertips against the ashy paper. And perhaps it was the case that the life that went from them, chased out by the fire and the light and the slow trickling of the successive years, had fled into the brute matter of the old world and given the objects their arrogance—yes, this was no life *ex nihilo*, but *their* life, the life that was missing from the empty-eyed children in front of him and their unluckier peers—the ones that the bitch shunted away in the night—because nothing in this world was lost or gained but simply moved from place to place, and there was nothing that anybody could do about it; and so the age of man was over and the age of rocks had begun.

The schoolmaster closed his eyes and his head fell forward onto his chest. The children began to wake up, pulling themselves from their desks and rubbing the sleep from their eyes. They looked over at the schoolmaster perched behind the book and the lectern, imprisoned by the warped red plastic bars of the baby chair and the weight of his robes, already losing his battle with sleep. The sun climbed higher. The light grew stronger. He roasted in his high chair and started to snore.

Agathe pushed herself away from the wall and crept past the rows of her brothers and sisters to the front of the classroom with the intention of looking into the schoolmaster's wrinkled face. The chickens clucked softly in the square outside. She could hear, too, the soughing of the wind as it passed through the forest and, somewhere in the distance, the reciprocal sigh of the mournful city. As she drew closer, Agathe noticed that moss was growing on the base of the schoolmaster's lectern. Had she ever dared approach him before? It occurred to her then that the unexpected return of Dolores had introduced a strange license into the slow dream of the schoolroom. Now that the schoolmaster was asleep the children were restless and excited. Behind Agathe they split into groups and began to speak in whispers, laughing and tossing their heads. She looked into the schoolmaster's face and observed the labial folds of his closed eyes, the parched skin with its labyrinth of broken blood vessels. Had there been a momentary quickening—a rush of life? Had it been them who had taken it from him, siphoning away at him as he slept? Slumped in his chair like that, the schoolmaster looked like an old rag, thrown aside. Agathe felt sorry for him and wanted to tell him so, but as she imagined twisting her fingers in his beard, she heard a shriek of laughter from the other side of the room and turned to look at her siblings. "See if you can stick it in her—then we'll know."— "Know what?"—"Whether she did it after all, dummy—"

They crouched around Dolores's desk—Adam, Franta, and Marek, and the girls too. Only Jakub kept his distance. Jan's children had already fled, accustomed as they were to the cruelty of their aunts and uncles and forever fearful of becoming its target. From up on the podium, Agathe was able to see over them, through the slight gap left between their blond heads and the brown wood of the desk to where Dolores cowered. It didn't surprise her, how quick the instinct was—the chewing out of the weak, the finding of holes. Dolores had always been hounded, in the schoolroom or at work in the field, and other times they'd wake her when it was still dark outside and then they would drag her to the ground and prod her and spit in her ears and sometimes they'd beat her until she blubbered for mercy. But these were beatings without consequence because Dolores never remembered what they'd done the next day, or if she did she never held it against her abusers. When morning came she'd still have the same confused smile pasted across her stupid lips and she'd crawl after Alexandra just like always and stick her backside out when Adam walked by. But now it was different. After an indeterminate time spent lurking at the boundaries of the camp, Dolores had dragged herself through the doorway to the rectangular dormitory that the younger children shared and during her slow, diurnal movement her siblings had watched her impassively: they neither loved her nor were glad to see her return, and only Agathe had regarded her sister with something other than this stony scrutiny. Dolores tried to slot herself back into the space she'd occupied before her departure, but despite the brevity of the interlude their arrangement had shifted. They had closed ranks against her and no pity could be expected from the usual quarters. Now the siblings clustered around Dolores. They had noticed the way she'd smiled as the schoolmaster had droned on with his fat palm laid flat against the book, stupidly, dreamily, wholly immersed in her interior world, whose rolling green hills and pleasantly soft clouds they couldn't even begin to imagine, where everyone communicated in the same inchoate mumble and pawed at each other with big dopey grins—they'd noticed it and had waited for the chance to lay into her, because there was something new in her that required a punishment greater than anything that had come before. What had she expected? The known and familiar suffering of the past; the usual cruelties. But under the desk, with the wall of her siblings enclosing her, she must have known that these were well and truly lost; that Marta, a long stick in her hand, would herald in a whole new era of pain. "There will be no help against evil."

The beatings of Dolores! There had been many. There would be many more. And if the schoolmaster were to put his dusty book to one side and crawl over to Dolores, use the trick of his learning to coax out the words before they died on her tongue, then he could gather from her soft, mumbled complaints material enough for a great jeremiad—he'd make good, like the chroniclers of the past, on the degradations of the present, because if more of them were to come, and the dead earth spring into life again, then certainly, certainly, they'd want to read all about Dolores and the moment that Marta slid under the desk with the stick in her hand, prolegomenon to future agonies.

Dolores covered her eyes with her big white hands. Marta pressed against her, a sloppy grin on her face, dark stains spreading across the thin fabric of her dress, damp with excitement. Adam stood up and pushed the desk away. In the sudden onslaught of the light Dolores cringed, silent save for one final whimper, and each of her siblings angled for a better view except for Jakub, who made for the door, shaking his head. Agathe stood on her tiptoes as Marta darted a snakish hand forward and lifted Dolores's skirt, exposing her puffy nether regions, and then a giggle rose up from the crowd and curled across the room to where the schoolmaster lay with his face in his beard. He grumbled and lifted his shaggy head and saw them there: the clump of children, the half-naked, terrified Dolores, who stared up at him with a plea in her eyes. The schoolmaster cleared his throat and slowly began to read. Agathe looked at Adam and then at Marta, who spat on Dolores and dropped the stick on the floor. The shadows withdrew.

* * *

In the dormitory that night Marta stood on her bed and sang in circles, long loops of made-up words, and try as they might her siblings were unable to catch the sense of anything that emerged from her mouth. She leaned drunkenly into Mary and the addition of her weight pushed her twin to one side so that the pair of them fell toward the mattress like two toppling boulders. The bed croaked beneath them, a sound that made Jakub wince and Agathe, who watched him without stopping, widen her eyes, and yet this loss of equilibrium did not stop Marta from singing—far from it—and she continued her tuneless song with an even greater effort of feeling; the sound of the thin, high voice that belied the physical solidity of her body trembled across the rectangular stone room in which her siblings lay, at least two or three of them to a bed, where they wrapped themselves around each other with the blind and indifferent need of whelps, so that viewed from above each bed contained a composite animal: a pink, fleshy chimera that panted in the heat rolling in through the open windows. Marta changed key. Now her voice was low and unsteady, and Jakub thought that she was singing about the city, that in her trembling song he could make out the contours of its ruins, the defeated buildings with their black mouths and tumbled walls, the broken cornices and the mossy faces above them that watched him as he walked through the silent streets without their mother's permission, his quick, disobedient mind darting against the wall of the past, and then he couldn't stand it any longer, the way it fluttered against his heart, and so he looked at his sister where she keeled in the arms of her twin and said in a sharp voice: "I'll make you be quiet if you don't stop." From the bed next to his, Dolores made a noise like a rooting pig. Since her return to the camp she had alternated between small, desperate sobs and this snuffling sound, which was sobbing's exhaustion, and it was clear to all of them that the Matriarch had not taken the unexpected return of her daughter well. Jakub jammed his fingers into his ears and buried his face in the dirty blanket. Adam, who had been lying on his stomach and pretending to sleep, turned over to look at him. "Please make her be quiet." How impossible it was to think in this room! Marta continued to wail, Franta hummed and hawed over the tool that he was repairing, while Eva, inexplicably asleep, began to snore. On the other side of the room Marek was tinkering away at the children's beloved television, which they had won from their mother at great cost and which was famously unreliable, and every small sound he made was implausibly magnified; from his position on the bed Jakub could hear the scrape of his brother's screwdriver as it twisted the metal screw, the tapping of his fingers on the cool glass screen, and the clatter made by a plastic panel as it hit the ground. These noises massed against his mind's border, meaning to find a way in, to make him like them, and then Jakub thought about the wall that cut him off from the rest of his siblings and whose preservation demanded a continual maintenance, because in the face of the general incoherence of their lives and the light no effort was too much, and he repeated his conclusion to himself in thoughts like explosions. Marta was growing more and more strident, drunk on her earlier success in the schoolroom but already too bored to see it through, even though now Dolores was unprotected and there was no risk of being interrupted. Jakub felt Agathe looking at him and wanted to hit her, but instead he pushed the woolen blanket hard into his closed eyes and imagined the wall, a black moat spreading out from its base and a sequence of ditches full of sharpened stakes.

But the others were inside his head—Franta's ugly face crumpled with concentration; the white string of spittle hanging from Marta's lips; the pale crabs of Dolores's hands; and Agathe's dumb stare—and then he opened his eyes, sat up, and began to look for his shoes. Marta stopped singing and said, "She'll be angry if she finds out you've left after dark," and Jakub scowled. "I don't care." The room was filled by the soft hum of something that was neither approval nor disapproval. Marta laughed—"You're mad!"— and Alexandra protested, "She'll find out—she'll find out and she'll get Jan to punish you." Agathe watched Jakub with her mouth open. He couldn't stand them nor the flat white disk of their expectation any longer, and so he strode down the aisle between the beds with the woolen blanket under one arm, opening the rusty metal door and stepping through it before they could say another word. Outside he was guided by the few blinking lamps that the Matriarch had had Jan install on the wall that encircled the encampment, despite his grumbling that it was a flagrant waste of energy;

over the years she had tried to create a system of patrols to go with them, and while her official pretense was that these hourly checks would alert them to the presence of any intruders, the children knew that she had simply wanted a means of knowing what they did when she wasn't looking. What possible threats could there be? The sending-away of Dolores was the first they had heard of another group, and nobody but the Matriarch claimed to have seen them, not even their uncle. The more skeptical of the siblings wondered, when they wondered at all, if it were simply the case that they were alone in a world that was utterly empty, clinging to the surface of a dead planet whose life was almost snuffed out entirely, whose carcass was dragged through the infinite wastes of an equally dead universe by forces that had no sympathy with them or any other living thing, that couldn't wait for it to be over! Jakub didn't need to ask the older members of the camp how it had gone in the years following the cataclysm. Their mother never tired of repeating it, as if what had happened had been nothing more than a chance for the Matriarch to prove her ingenuity, who thinking to repopulate the world by dint of will had seen the beginning of a new civilization, this time leaving nothing to chance, everything contingent on her, spreading out from her tireless body in concentric circles of increasing perfection.

The Matriarch's other story went like this: A deadening wind swept from the epicenter of some secret and unnamed disaster and the people had sickened, slipping away from the world in droves. A shadow fell across the land. The shadow had no name; the shadow was *white*, and it was this pale shadow that had crooked the world. He could see the faint parabola of the descent in his mind's eye: they skidded into a littoral eternity where time was meaningless and progress unimaginable, the end even more so. It was an event that the other adults remembered only glancingly, that couldn't be caught with the muddied words of a language that was broken too, and so they hid themselves from it in the shell of the present and drew back from their memories with startled turtle eyes. Only the Matriarch had been determined to see the empty world as an opportunity. But even she had grown tired; the security efforts had mumbled out. Now only the erratic and infrequent wanderings of their uncle broke the quiet contempt of the night, a torch balanced in the claw of his hand. Tonight the encampment was as deserted as always, and Jakub passed through the gate unhindered and entered the silent forest where the trees closed ranks around him. In the past this had been a road, he thought, picking his way along the crumbling line of tarmac that led to the city, until the forest had absorbed its tributary streets and isolated its body. The weeds had made inroads in the porous stone, the roots had followed them, and then the bloodless road had truly died, drying up into the memorial of itself. Yet it wasn't over, though the forest waited and the trees conspired among themselves and the animals bided their time. The road still led to the city and the city still stood. Before long it began to rise up on both sides: the black lines of the apartment blocks interrupted the canopy and the forest was cut through with the suggestion of streets; he could see, too, the old cars hunched up in the dark like dying animals, and dotted within the undergrowth the even darker rectangles of doors and windows. As he walked by, the cracked red plastic of a headlamp grinned at him from the undergrowth. The shapes of the city were sketched out by the steady light of the moon, but in the distance there was another kind of light, still faint, that danced at the edge of his vision before darting away again. It was a leaf-shaped shard of some greater light buried within the schoolmaster's building that knifed away at the surrounding darkness. A ray shattered itself against the broken glass of the window and was thrown into the forest—it was this that he'd seen, and Jakub wondered how the schoolmaster could bear it, because if the yellow light summoned the dead world for Jakub, whose knowledge of it was secondary, inherited, then surely it would pain the old schoolmaster, no matter how vacant his little black heart. But in the end how much did Jakub know about what would pain the schoolmaster and what wouldn't? Although the schoolmaster had as little as possible to do with the encampment, not bothering to hide his contempt for either the Matriarch or her children, in time Jakub had worn him down and the schoolmaster had relinquished his mysterious silence in favor of a high, hateful babble full of reasons and repudiations, pivoting around the room on his thick, powerful arms, condemning the present, their mother's dream, and shaking the past until it screamed, and Jakub had discovered that the schoolmaster hated the Matriarch even more than he did, with a dark and starless passion that knew no pauses, the discovery of which had surprised the blond boy because his own hatred was erratic, contingent. He wanted to know more about the past that the three adults shared, and so night after night he returned to the city and the schoolmaster to ask about the university where his uncle had studied theology, or the derelict castle crouching on its solitary hill, or even about other cities languishing by other rivers in other lands, but despite his best efforts the schoolmaster's memory was blank.

When Jakub finally emerged from the cover of the trees, the light was lying flat on the stony ground before the small rectangular window that opened into the schoolmaster's basement room. He shook his head—how different it was from the blind white light of the day!—and walked through the door to the apartment block and along the dark passage that led down to the lower level. When he entered the room the schoolmaster was on the floor, his black robes spilling around him. The light came from a small metal desk lamp that he occasionally lifted, like a torch, to inspect a heaping mound of fabric so big that it dwarfed the legless schoolmaster. He turned his head to look at the boy standing in the middle of the room and said nothing. Jakub held out the woolen blanket. "I have something for you." If only it was that easy to get at his heart—the schoolmaster didn't blink. "Stupid boy." But when Jakub tossed the blanket into the center of the room, the schoolmaster pounced. The lamp clattered to one side and his robes, lifted into the air by the sudden movement, flapped around his missing lower half. As the schoolmaster scrabbled across the concrete floor toward the dirty blanket, Jakub looked at the mound. It towered above them both, a mountain of rotting cloth capped with lenticular shadow that had long since broken through the basement ceiling and penetrated the upper rooms of the apartment block. He turned back to the schoolmaster, who was cradling the blanket in his dusty arms, and said, "If it wasn't for me you wouldn't have hardly any fabric at all." The schoolmaster had been collecting fabric for as long as any of them could remember and Jakub had helped him, roaming through the ruined city and bringing the schoolmaster old blankets and coats, duvet covers and sofa stuffing, wadded towels, sheaths of tarpaulin, anything and everything that he found. This had been the pretext he had needed to leave the camp and his siblings for the city, and in doing so he had become different from them. He had understood at last the enormity of their isolation: the solitude of dark rooms where the dust was as thick as the snow that came every winter, the crumbling apartment blocks riddled with green ivy, the suspended time of the black roads with their crusting of rusty automobiles. The past, like a great carcass, stretched out before him. There was no reckoning it! The schoolmaster hauled himself closer to the mound and placed the blanket on the dark slope that rose up above his head. Meanwhile he talked to himself in a gruff and resentful mutter that was meant to be heard: "Stupid boy! Mind broken like the rest of them. Why do you keep coming here? Every day sometimes. Too often. Don't you have sisters to fuck, progeny to create . . ." but Jakub didn't care because he knew that the schoolmaster's desire to be rid of him was part of his desire to be rid of everything, a total renunciation, away and done with it all, the world, the city, the encampment, their mother, their uncle, Jakub and his brothers and sisters and even ox-eyed Dolores, for whom the schoolmaster had a soft spot. And once these preliminaries were over the schoolmaster would speak to him and Jakub would be distracted, however briefly, from the monotony of the encampment and the dull immensity of the waiting night, and so he concentrated on a whorl of the schoolmaster's dark hair and waited for the muttering to end. He thought about Dolores and examined his motives. Had he come to the city because he had wanted to talk about Dolores with the schoolmaster? The Matriarch's sudden decision, the sending-away and the equally unexpected return? Suddenly Jakub was desperate. "I wanted to talk to you—" The schoolmaster interrupted him. "If you were good, then you'd bring me fabric and expect nothing in return—you'd bring me fabric out of the goodness of your good heart." He looked back at Jakub over his chubby shoulder. "But you're as rotten as the rest of them!" Jakub agreed, echoing his words. "As rotten as the rest of them!"

The schoolmaster turned back to the mound. "I'm building a cocoon. And when I've finished, I'll climb inside and sleep until I wake up in a different world with a different body. Away from those squalling brats and you. Why are you here?" He paused and licked his dry lips. "Don't you have sisters to fuck?" Jakub pretended not to hear him. "Won't you suffocate in there?" The schoolmaster scowled. "Old questions. You know I won't. I'm building a machine. You don't understand but you'll see. I'll be immortal." He picked up the lamp and aimed the light at the mound. Now Jakub could see that it was heaving with activity: every surface was covered with a layer of golden moths that twitched and fluttered their wings as the light bounced off them. It struck him then that the mound was something living, thrown up from the earth, something that grew in fits and bursts; although he himself had fed it, the mound was independent, bent on thriving. If the schoolmaster thought that it was a vehicle for salvation he was mistaken, Jakub decided, because the mound was for itself only. But the schoolmaster would never realize his error; their world was assailed by an endless dreaming, carried in by the bright light of the shapeless days, which in the end had taken even the Matriarch unawares. The schoolmaster had already turned back to the mound. "The light won't be able to reach me in there. I collected fabric—*you* collected fabric for me—enough to form an absolute barrier. And nothing can slip through it except for them, my brothers and sisters. It will be God's mound." The schoolmaster licked his lips again. "The outer layers of the mound will be as dry and as parched as the desert at noon. Nothing will grow there because unlike in the desert here there is no light, so the outer layers of the mound will also be as cold and as lifeless as the moon. But it will be warm and moist at the heart of the mound. The heat will protect me from the winter and keep my siblings alive and we'll talk together. The mound will be a community; the mound will be a new city. I've told you this before."

Jakub looked into the schoolmaster's sweaty face. "But you aren't a moth." The schoolmaster dismissed him. "Haven't I told you enough about the transformative power of faith? Look at your sisters. Look at that bitch that you call a mother. The old laws were washed away with everything else; I should teach you that at school. The camp, your mother, the children—the borders are collapsing. If only some flood!— but there will be a flood, another flood. It was simply the case that the last one wasn't strong enough, or the one before it, and then it will truly be over and the saved—the cocooned—will emerge from their slumber at the same time as the changed God, in His new image. They say that God has left us, but He is simply sleeping. He dreams, *you* are His nightmare, but this won't last—a new era is coming." A shudder passed over his mammoth torso and the schoolmaster looked up at the enormous mound with love in his beady black eyes. "God isn't a moth," Jakub laughed, closer to him now. The schoolmaster ignored him. "He can't hear me because He is inside His cocoon. Swaddled up in the divine cloth. Growing, changing! He can't hear any of us. One day you'll all see. I will be set loose by my creator: He will unhusk me. I will fly into a new sky that will be black, not white at all—I will fly behind the winged God into the infinite darkness of the new heavens." Jakub touched the metal of the lamp with his fingers. The heat burned him. The schoolmaster dug his hands into his beard and pulled out a fistful of hair. "These, too. I add myself to the mound. It is necessary for the soul to be proportioned to the body." He darted a suspicious glance at Jakub. "I've told you this before." Jakub looked at the schoolmaster and shrugged. "Dolores has come back . . ." The dark bulk of the schoolmaster eclipsed the beam of the lamp. The mound, the wall, his mother's dream . . . She had embarrassed herself, thrown Dolores away for nothing. The schoolmaster hadn't heard him. He repeated himself, "Dolores has come back . . ." and then the schoolmaster began to spit it out, his old monologue with almost nothing changed: "Her project has failed, but that's no surprise! I knew it would fail, from the very moment she told me what she intended to do. No God, no science! I said to her: How are you going to do it like that? I offered myself to her! She said no, of course, the stuck-up bitch. And it began with a lie, anyway, because she was always with her brother; she was always too close to her brother. People would whisper about them, even before it happened. She was glad to have him, away from the others, from the university, everything she'd hated. When his wife began to die, she saw her chance." Jakub stopped him. "I don't care about that—what she did with him!" The schoolmaster smiled and then said quietly to himself, "He doesn't like it when I talk about *siblings*!" Jakub didn't reply, but the schoolmaster looked at him with a gleam in his cockroach eye and decided not to let go. "Dolores coming back . . . Well, what's left to say? As if the earth would spring into life again. As if she could fix it in her *own way*, because she'd never want the past back, not your mother, but a new world, one that could finally revolve around her. Selfish cow!" The schoolmaster pulled himself up to his full height and glared at Jakub. "You're all rotten!" He paused and thought about it. "Even then I dreamed of my cocoon." No longer sure what he had expected from the stubborn schoolmaster, Jakub mumbled something rude in the broken Czech that the children spoke when they were alone. The schoolmaster hissed, "Don't speak like that! Do you want to wake it up? Yes, the city. It sleeps, like God in the cloth, wrapped in darkness. Don't wake it up!" Jakub laughed. "They can't hear us. They're all dead."

The schoolmaster shot the lamplight into the heart of the mound. "They are waiting for Him: for the God-moth to come and wrap them up in His wings. They are waiting for you to die." Jakub rubbed at his eyes. "It's impossible to talk to you!" The schoolmaster turned and spat a glob of phlegm toward the mound, and Jakub thought to himself that the city wasn't sleeping at all, but listening, hanging on their every word; he dreamed of a vast intelligence hidden inside the ruined city center, buried in the dirt, the mulch of civilization, pinned down by structures that could no longer bear their own weight, an enormous and compromised citadel of trash. A white whale in the darkness; something that belonged to the old world. The schoolmaster knew what it was called but wouldn't tell him. The lamplight beatified him, bounced off his toothy grin, and for a moment Jakub wanted to cry, looking at the mound and the schoolmaster slumped beside it like a silly old doll.

The next day was a Saturday, and, as the Matriarch kept to the old calendar, that morning nobody went for the schoolmaster. By noon the sun flooded through even the densest parts of the canopy, and when Jan came scowling toward them the children nodded wearily because they knew that there was nowhere else to hide. They pulled themselves up from the grass by the schoolroom and followed him through the forest, snapping at his heels like a pack of dogs. Soon the field stretched out before them, a terrible flat plain, immobile in the baking light. A few insects buzzed lazily across it, but aside from this the field and the forest that surrounded it were silent. Their older sisters were already working in the distance. Agathe pushed at the dirt with the tip of her boot. The spring had been hot, so hot she didn't understand how anything could grow or what it was that Jan was planning, but this was the gap between the younger and older siblings, who were industrious and capable of holding intentions across the drowsy days, weeks, months, and years. What was there to do? Jan carried it in his mind. First they would break up the soil with rusting pickaxes, electric power being so scarce in the camp that the agriculture of the present was largely that of the distant past, relying, as it did, on the brute force of bodies. It had taken Jan many years to clear the field, cutting down the trees and pulling the stumps from the earth with the help of Marketa, Tereza, Adela, and the others, and a sputtering red tractor that caused as many problems as it solved. Poring over old agricultural magazines, faded copies of *Farmář*, he had not given in to despair but had coolly assessed their situation and its limits and decided that the ancient methods were the most reliable. Whatever belonged to the past that he had heard about in the Matriarch's stories was broken; he could not get it back, no matter how its promises tormented him—*Molekulární genetika pro šlechtění nejen na dojivost! Intenzita v obilninách se vyplatí! Dýně pro krásu i pro chuť!*—and so he had turned to another past for answers, an even older past, and his field was divided into three in the ancient way, a holy number, and at night he tossed and turned and dreamed of long, purposeful strips of land, and of growth, endless growth, a field as big as the city and the forest razed. In the end Jan's field was not only a field but the record of his history and the shape of his desire, the impenetrable interiority that even his mother couldn't get at, everything secret inside him that was uniquely *Jan*, and it didn't matter that his siblings tracked all over it with their dirty, clopping feet, because nobody would ever understand the field like he did, or share his delight in the way that the tortured earth renewed itself, plenishing to green. And lastly the field was testament to effort, a monumental effort, because the creation of the field—and try as he might Jan could never see it as anything but a slow, methodical *building*—had been accomplished alongside the maintenance of the camp, the sending out of foraging parties to the suburbs in pursuit of supplies, canned food, clothes, and medicines, and, of course, the upholding of the law, the Matriarch's law, which could never be neglected, because if it were then chaos would slink in, Jan had visioned it, a sly, slippery chaos that waited at the wall of their world for a gap to slip through, for Jan to be off guard. Yes, he was proud of his field, the first field of the new world, from which others would surely follow. It was a foothold of a kind. For ten years now the field had offered up its bounty: rye, oats, potatoes, broad beans, and rows of green lettuce. But the field was a wooden citadel; the slightest mistake could destroy it, the smallest wavering of his attention. *My kingdom for an ox!* thought Jan, with nothing close to a laugh in his leathery heart. He caught sight of Marta, hanging back with Jakub and Marek, and scowled.

As the siblings crowded by the grassy bank that overlooked the field, Jan began to give them their instructions for the afternoon. Agathe closed her eyes. Somewhere beyond the place where the dirt path vanished into the forest Dolores was still crawling, unable to catch up with them. When she got there they would harness her up like one of the big, lumbering animals from the schoolmaster's books, and Dolores would pull the wooden plow through the soil, her pale skin reddening with its weight. No—it would be too much for her; although they would poke her and prod her and call her names, she wouldn't move an inch, the plow falling forward and sinking into her soft shoulders; a white leviathan, smoking in the heat. It was no use. When Agathe opened her eyes again the field yawned before her and Dolores was nowhere to be seen. Jan grunted and waved them in the direction of the shed to the left of the field where the tools were kept, sweltering in the only remaining crescent of shadow. As she walked toward it, Agathe could sense Adam behind her and threw a cautious look over her shoulder. He caught her eye and smiled, but before she could try to respond, Marta and Mary were shoving past them with hoes in their hands. Agathe ducked inside, grabbed one of the pickaxes, and slouched back into the light. She walked into the bright field. It had seemed impossible that anything could grow in what the schoolmaster called the "incomprehensible ruin of the earth" and yet every year a line of green crops emerged from the dark soil into the light, and these were encouraged to grow by every means possible. It was true, even the schoolmaster had to admit it, that Jan's crops were a necessary addition to the canned food they scavenged from the desolated suburbs and then hoarded in the upper rooms of their mother's apartment block; yes, even the schoolmaster, who hated Jan as much as Agathe hated Dolores, had had to admit that the oldest of the Matriarch's children was useful in his own leathery way, and so it continued, this second cultivation of the earth. Dolores wouldn't come at all, Agathe decided, sweating as she swung the pickaxe into the dirt. As usual something would distract her, and then the whole of it—the insinuating trees, the encroaching undergrowth—would shuffle into her empty skull and take root; she'd never make it all the way out to the field, and, as she was no use anyway, Jan wouldn't miss her. She watched her older sisters toiling at the field's farthest edge, like gulls in a brown sea. They were flocked by their own children, who resembled not Jan but his younger siblings, many of them, like Dolores and Agathe, lacking some limb or quality: they were born without hands, feet, legs, or the upper portion of their lips, and were prone to strange fits and visions, moody and withdrawn. From her position on the opposite side of the field, it seemed to Agathe that each sister was a planet around which revolved many moons, none of which could be expected to attain the size and dignity of the planet itself; instead these were weak, hopeless copies, burning with borrowed light. By the time Agathe looked up again the day had moved on: the sun crawled back down to the earth and the field was striped with javelins of light and the dark shadows of the trees. Above her the sky blazed yellow and orange. Her own siblings were deep into the field, and now Jan and the older sisters followed in their tracks, burying their blades in the dirt. Their lips were moving, and it didn't matter that Agathe couldn't hear what they were saying because she knew how it would go. They were cursing their mother and the light and whatever it was that tied them to the earth, because in this heat nobody cared about staying alive, and whatever dim loyalty it was that tied them to her schemes was gone, as wilted as the rest of it.

She decided to give up. After making sure that none of

the others were watching her, Agathe dropped to the ground and lay flat on the earth. If only someone would come and talk to her! Not a sibling but a stranger, as if the world were not as empty as the Matriarch had claimed before the onset of a new dream. When Agathe squinted she could almost see them walking across the field, some of them hooded and robed against the light in the schoolmaster's custom, and some as bareheaded as her family, too far gone to care. They would sleep with her older siblings, and children, new children, would be born into the encampment, and these would be better than the children they birthed on their own, who belonged to the poisoned earth and the doomed union of brother and sister. If only they weren't alone! It was a similar desperation that had led to the disastrous sending-away of Dolores, she thought, the first effort from their mother to contact another group, even though by now Agathe was sure that the suggestion of a marriage had emerged from nowhere save the Matriarch's lonely head. But in the presence of these imaginary strangers their mother's despair would intensify because the stories they would tell her were about a world that was dead, dead, dead, the same nothing wherever they went. They would stay long enough to get a real eyeful of the encampment and then they would chalk the experience up beside their other experiences of the ruined world, not the thing they hoped to find, and be on their way again, searching for a sign that they hadn't been forgotten after all. And although they would praise the lie of the camp, just as they had praised other efforts in the past, with lies of their own, they would be unable to conceal their dismay from her sharp eyes, and the Matriarch would know that what she did with her brother had no higher purpose, was nothing other than the vainglorious impulse of her own rotten heart. A hundred tiny groups, clinging to life—*If only some flood*—! Agathe lay on the ground with her face in the dirt and listened to the sun comb indifferently over the field. Even with her stone's reasoning she knew that things would get worse from here.

✳ ✳ ✳

"Dolores coming back—" he rasped, "can't not say it, have to say it, very *unwise* move—" Then the delicate spasming of his long fingers. "Did you speak to the girl?"

The darkness of the room was cool, soothed her soul, and now her nightmares were locked beneath the abyssal glass of the computer screen; in only a few hours Jan would oversee the turning off of the power, and then the matter would be out of her hands, the matter of the day, that was, and the Matriarch could turn her attention to other things, perhaps even fall backward into the chasm of herself and let the problems of the camp drip from her mind. But now all she wanted was a moment of peace. Sitting in the dusty red armchair opposite, her brother wouldn't let her go. He peered across at her with his wide, glassy eyes and repeated himself: "Did you speak to the girl?" The Matriarch adjusted her sunglasses. "She was cold and frightened. She wasn't sure how she had gotten back. Something happened." Their uncle continued to stare. "I left her at the designated place." "Something happened that frightened her," the Matriarch hedged, but their uncle was having none of it. "It will get worse. Hate to say it. It will get much worse now that they are involved." The Matriarch wasn't sure which *they* he meant, and so she said nothing. His eyes darted around her body but found no weakness. "It was *your* idea to make contact with them." The Matriarch looked at him through her black lenses. "Everything is always my idea." Their uncle straightened up in his chair, and the handkerchief that covered his head, bald save for a few wispy strands of dirty blond hair, wimpled, be-nunning him—his heart primmed up against her. For a while neither of them said anything. It was true that the return of Dolores meant nothing good for them, but the Matriarch was not yet certain whether it was the disaster that her brother insisted. If the others were real, then they would come for Dolores and there was no telling whether they would be angry or not. And if the others weren't real and no consequences were forthcoming, then her brother was right, her children would be on the alert, having spotted her weakness, because as far as their mother was concerned, belief, an absolute, unwavering belief, was the true premise of the encampment. To slip once! No, she had been slipping for years; for a long time Jan had been the family's true manager—all the Matriarch had was a handful of symbols. Yet some of them remembered how it had been, the suggestion of her love. They continued to uphold her law, and as she watched the encampment from her office window the children followed the paths she had carved out for them. They raked earth, planted seeds, pumped water from deep underground wells, sewed clothes, fed chickens, collected fuel—the biblical cadence of their actions astounded her, and even Dolores trundled into the future—but all that she had gained could be lost in an instant.

There was a sense, too, in which the Matriarch was still wrapped up in her dream; she was brimming with something light and foul that once she might have called hope. On that morning when she had woken with her head full of what she had believed to be a *message*, she had thought she could see it too, the schoolmaster's imaginary tower, only now it gleamed bright and benevolent, a signal leaping over the forest. She had managed to extract very little from Dolores, who had wobbled before her with that choiceless, wordless genuflection so ubiquitous among the legless of her children, the Matriarch watching her from the throne of her chair, damp fingers clenching slightly against the fake leather of the armrests. From her burbling emerged only certain *images*, nothing concrete: a man who had pushed her; the scrape of roots and small stones against her white, fleshy thighs; the earthy smell of the forest floor . . . Her brother repeated himself, "It was your idea—*everything* was your idea," and something moved in the dark corridor behind him—Jan was listening to them, waiting for the Matriarch's next command, only she had no idea what it would be. She felt her system spinning away from her. "Maybe nothing will happen." But even as she said it, she knew it wasn't true. Looking at her brother, the Matriarch couldn't remember what it was she had known or had felt, as if the light and the forest and the city had finally breached her walls, filling her with false notions. As the years went by, her thoughts had loosened, so imperceptibly at first that for some time the

Matriarch had not been aware of any change, but now she saw a great river split into thin, winding distributaries whose courses she could not follow. More and more often she could not understand her own reasoning. She was wracked by indecision—the hands that rested in her lap were limp and sweaty. Even if she wasn't sure what would happen next, a wind swept in from the city that let her know that fate was sharpening its knives. It would have been better if Dolores hadn't come back. It would have been better if she had starved in the forest, because as she crawled across the dusty square her bright body was a challenge to the Matriarch's vision that none of them could ignore. Still—the children had no way of proving her wrong; the city was between the encampment and her fantasy, at least that was something. And was it wrong to have dreamed of another group afflicted by the same pain, the empty city, the poisoned river, the unbearable whiteness of the new chemical sky? For once she had wanted to have faith, just like her brother, in something beyond herself. But in sending Dolores away the Matriarch understood that she had been driven by something secret and shameful—loneliness. She had bowed beneath the weight of her burden, her brother was right; loneliness had driven her to it. She had dreamed of an alliance, of a mutual sharing of responsibility, and this was the trick of their era, that thought and fact could so easily become the same thing. Had the Matriarch misled herself? It was impossible to know. All she could be certain of was that she had felt something so strongly that she had been incapable of resisting it and that this in itself was a lessening of her powers. Now something had gone wrong, and although she didn't blame

Dolores, couldn't blame her vague, terrified daughter, only fold her into the wings of her arms, the Matriarch could see her system falling to pieces. In the black space of her mind she fumbled for her spreadsheets. If Jan was loyal to her, along with the older members of her brood, the same could not be said for their younger siblings, Jakub, Adam, Marek, and Marta, and Jan's children, who already almost outnumbered her own. What did they want? Her computer screen was dark, but she was able to consult those long columns of information anyway, inwardly scrolling through her notes and observations about the children and their activities, and yet, as she had never been able to bring herself to record anything that might confirm the doubts she had locked away inside the cabinet of her mind, it was the case that her records were useless to her now, and, realizing that she had only ever seen what she had wanted to see, the Matriarch felt another one of those unpleasant jolts that had plagued her ever since the unfortunate return of her daughter. It was possible that the children hated her. It was possible that they wanted her dead. The sound of their uncle coughing pulled her back from her thoughts.

"I was thinking. You're right. It was my idea. Though I had good reasons for taking a risk." Their uncle said, "That old song again." "We have to survive," she replied. Jan scuffled in the doorway. The light that came in through the window played across her brother's face and reminded her that once he had been as handsome as Jakub; young, definite. A cloud passed over the sun and his cheek became a basin of shadow. "Is it that certain?" Again the Matriarch was an impregnable fortress, an active star. She leaned forward in her chair and said, "Yes. You want to give up and die, but I won't let you. I know what you think—you and the schoolmaster. It's intolerable, that attitude. We have to keep on going." Her brother looked at her and smiled. "It was your idea to try something different." Only the black surface of her sunglasses answered him, and so he leaned back in his chair and distanced himself from her problems, his breath scuttling from his open mouth. The Matriarch was already changing direction—if the others were real, then perhaps she had sabotaged herself by sending them Dolores and not one of her other daughters, though at the time she hadn't seen it that way, had been won over by that wonderful passivity; or maybe it was that all along she had been holding her cards close to her chest, and, doubting the substantiality of her dream, had been willing only to sacrifice a daughter who was more disposable than the rest. She had never had enough faith. And if her daughter had failed her, it was because the Matriarch had been keeping something back. A terrible guilt came over her and the soft wheezing of her brother was no ward against it. The Matriarch gave him up and turned to Jan, waiting in the doorway. "Bring me Dolores." Her desire—he was so tuned to it that he was on the move before she finished speaking.

Outside, the sun was beginning to descend, slathing the square in red fire. But Jan was not afraid of the light, though he shielded his eyes with his hand as he emerged from his mother's office, and nor was he afraid of the younger children and the way they looked at him as he set their tasks before them and explained the necessity of their routine, what he liked to call, without irony, "the daily grind." Ingrates, all of them, incapable of understanding; having grown up within this system—*his* system—they had no memory of the brutality of the early days, before clean water, regular food, electrical power, and the efficient disposal of waste, the situation into which Jan himself had been born and had thrown himself into fixing—when they shook their heads at the disorder all around them, the silenced machinery of the dead world, themselves discarded, dolled with wonder. The *confusion*—that was it, what the brats couldn't understand—the *confusion*, the *chaos*; and death, waiting at the margins, shape-shifting. The clean lines of the camp and the clockwork beauty of their work—they couldn't value it! Jan huffed and made his way down the steps that led to the square and the schoolroom, and the sun eyed him up, hunting for an opportunity to lead him astray and prevent him from carrying out the Matriarch's order. But his mind was encased in amber, the hardened sap of his love for her, and he was not like the others, not given to looseness or the drifting of intention. He crossed the square with brisk, decisive steps. There was no pattern to Dolores's movements, Jan remembered, because her bird-brain was incapable of following any routine or retaining instructions, and so she spent each night in a different bed, attaching herself to the sibling who'd been the least cruel to her that day, but now that even Alexandra had betrayed her it was likely that Dolores would be where her younger siblings were not—Jan had not failed to notice their new hostility toward her, how they laughed and kicked at her as she passed them by—and so either Dolores would be sheltering in one of the empty hospital buildings or she would be with his sisters, who took pity on her, having vague, terrified children of their own. Jan decided that he would first look for Dolores among the mothers and young children, and he could picture her already, ovoid in the dark, a cuckoo's egg . . . Yes, he would look for her there because really she was one of those children, a big, stupid baby, incapable of understanding anything, least of all the extent to which she had disappointed them. Jan walked along the path with his head down. His sisters lived in a crumbling four-story complex to the eastern side of the camp with their children, and even if Dolores was nowhere to be found, there would be no harm in looking in and seeing them, *his* sisters, who were hardworking and reliable, nothing like the younger ones. Dolores! If the Matriarch wanted her, Jan concluded, it would be to punish her, kick her around until she coughed up more information—the stupid little bitch—always creating problems, couldn't even get fucked right—and then maybe their mother would finally put her straight, send her packing for good. Because if the others were to come, then his precious order would be broken, and so the not-fucking of Dolores would ruin everything that he, Jan, had worked so hard to build.

By the time that he reached their building Jan was fuming with resentment and his big sun-scoured face was twisted in a scowl that meant nothing good for Dolores. He wanted to make his mother happy, complete her order, but also to hurt Dolores, to beat her until she screamed for having dared to err so grievously. "That bitch, that lump," he sang to himself as he marched into his sisters' quarters. Inside only the thinnest ribbons of light came through the boarded-up windows, and his sisters appeared before him in a soft green haze. The slow sleepiness of the room was almost more than he could bear with the longing in his heart, but Jan was resolute, his mother's face in his mind. "Has anyone seen Dolores?" he asked, and one of the children laughed. A female voice—he thought it was Adela—answered him, "Marketa. She's with Marketa—upstairs," and even as the room slipped back into the same soft silence Jan kept on muttering to himself, "That bitch, that lump," because he was not to be derailed from his mission, not by a whole host of sisters, and so he walked through the dim entrance hall and climbed the stairs that led to the upper floors. He found Dolores in one of the bedrooms on the second floor, curled around Marketa like an enormous parasite as the pair slept fitfully on the bobbled mattress, and for a moment he simply stood and watched them, Marketa tossing and turning and Dolores snuffling into her like an enormous pig. When Dolores rolled over Jan was ready for her; scowling, he kicked the blunt steel toe of his boot into the soft mush of his younger sister's ribs, and Dolores awoke with a painful expulsion of breath, too winded to scream, her mouth opening and closing with the stunned gasping of a fish. "Lump. Pig." Marketa didn't wake up. Dolores looked at Jan and the plea in her eyes irritated him even more. Why had the Matriarch chosen her above all of the others? Dolores hadn't done the job. She had disobeyed their mother, and soon the strangers would come for her, big men unchanged by the light, their faces smooth like Jakub's, and they would throw his poor, gentle sisters down on the dry earth and fuck them from behind while their children watched, and Jan wouldn't be able to lift a finger to stop them because he'd be stuck underneath Dolores and the soft monstrosity of her rear end, her stumps pinning his torso to the ground; he would watch as the others fucked his sisters, *his* sisters, and it would all be her fault.

Their mother was waiting, but Jan didn't care. He kicked Dolores again and she slid away from Marketa. As he walked toward his sister she began to struggle across the dusty stone floor on her fat sausage arms, too slow to get away—and could something like her ever really *escape*?—and then Jan knelt down beside Dolores and grabbed her face so that he could look into her eyes and see if anything within those vague depths changed as he fucked her, his other hand clawing at the elastic of her waistband. Her lips were parted and he could see the wet red mass of her tongue. He pulled off her skirt and hauled the abbreviated lump of her body toward him. Yes, there was something like fear in those strange eyes, so different from theirs, like Agathe's. Behind them, Marketa moaned, still asleep. Again, Jan saw his sisters in the mud; if only they had sent some other sister, or had let him at her first, because Jan would have taught her then like he was teaching her now. Outside the sun plunged lower in the sky, and Dolores really was wailing as he fucked her and the blood from her broken hymen splattered across his shirt; he was aware of Marketa somewhere behind him, hitting his back with her fists, but the more Dolores screamed the better he felt—a pleasure as vast as the city, washing over the dead stone buildings—and then Jan cried out as he came and pushed Dolores away from him. Exhausted, he looked down at his younger sister. Marketa leaned over his shoulder and looked too. "Poor Dolores." Her thighs were clamped together, and something about the thin black line between them made Jan think about chicken flesh pimpling in the air, post-slaughter nudity; blood, feathers. No, he wouldn't feel bad. It was Dolores's fault for coming back and for having those *legs*, the way they terminated above the knee, the mighty thighs loose and passive, trembling with vulnerability. It would have been better for everyone if she'd died in the forest. Now Dolores cowered before him on the dark stone floor and Jan's heart was empty. He leaned forward and grabbed her hair, which was longer than he remembered, and climbed up onto his feet. Her hair was a rope, a pale rope in his clenched fist, and when he yanked it Dolores responded with a low sob before following his movement, crawling behind him as he made his way back along the corridor toward the stairs, leaving Marketa on her mattress, where, Jan knew, she would soon fall asleep again, because there could be no event singular enough to disturb their routine, least of all the wailings and lamentations of a stuck pig. He led Dolores through the dim rooms of their quarters and as she wept his children lined up to watch them, laughing, and Jan felt like Zeus with his Io, careering through the earthly wastes, but of course he was in the service of something much greater than his own desire, and this thing was his mother, their mother, the mother of everything around them, and how had the schoolmaster phrased it—"a fair field full of folk"?—Dolores was his cow and she stumbled behind him along the sun-drenched plain of his memory, tripping from past to present to future and back again, the yoke around her neck, and the rest of them, too, a whole field of penitents, stumbling together, and somewhere above it all their mother watched them through her impenetrable black lenses.

The light brought him back to himself, made him define himself against the sudden onslaught of radiance. Dolores winced as the sun hit her face and Jan interpreted the slight tugging of her hair in his hand as resistance; he pulled her forward with a wrench that made her scream. As she tumbled into the dirt Jan noticed that she was still half-naked and unease roiled up in his belly—would the Matriarch care? He kicked her again and his sister rolled onto her back as if she were too weary to defend herself. Next Jan knelt down beside her and spat on his sleeve and tried to wipe the blood away from her thighs. "Because of the heat—she'll think you're naked because of the heat, and you'll nod if she asks you. It's exactly the kind of stupid, shameless thing you'd do—to go around like that in front of all your brothers and sisters. Who'd want to fuck you, anyway—it's your fault, you made me do it because you behaved so badly. If you do anything other than nod, I'll kill you." Dolores stared up at the sky and Jan watched her for a little longer, waiting to see if her expression would change, and when it didn't, having identified no signs of rebellion, he looked away again, satisfied. She hadn't understood anything; there was no danger. Jan walked down the path with Dolores dragging herself along at his side. He felt the emptiness of the encampment, or the world, mound up around him, and so he walled himself against it and concentrated on the rhythm of their movement—the carrying out of his mother's order, his anticipation of tasks to come, the as-yet-unproven structure of the night that lay before him, and the endless sequence of days following hard on its heels; all these things came together in the hard brown nut of his mind, his eyes bunched up against the light, until something like a sigh from Dolores told him that they were there already and the apartment block in which his mother brooded stood before them with sorrow in its black windows. Jan pulled his sister up the steps that led to the stone platform in front of the Matriarch's office, and when they entered the corridor a voice slithered out from under her closed door, a guttural whisper that crashed over him like the sea, summoning memories of earlier times, indistinct times, when Jan had been part of her and she had been part of him. On hearing his mother's voice, Jan was suddenly overcome with a feeling of shame—yes, it could only be called *shame*—and Dolores, poor, deflowered Dolores, surged down the short corridor toward their mother's door with unusual speed, too quick for Jan—her hair slipped through his fingers, loose with remorse—and scrabbled at the metal with her stubby nails, a whine in her throat. The whispering stopped, and he heard their uncle climb up from his sagging armchair and walk toward the door. Listening to those slow, deliberate footsteps, Jan imagined his mother's expression on seeing the clearly defiled Dolores and a kind of agony rushed through him, because deep down he knew that the Matriarch loved each and every one of her children, even Dolores and Agathe, and he in turn loved her for her gentleness, her magnanimity of spirit. Dolores wobbled by the door, a naked reprimand. What had he been thinking, losing control like that? A strip of light appeared on the floor beside him. Their uncle darted his small head out from behind the door and squinted at them through his spectacles. "It's Jan with Dolores," he said so that his sister could hear him. "I only want to see Dolores," the

Matriarch replied, and Jan's ugly face crumpled with rejection. Their uncle looked at him without saying anything, his blue eyes calm. Jan hesitated at the margins of her presence, and then spun on his heel and dashed away. The brightness swallowed him up.

Their uncle pushed the door open all the way and Dolores lugged her big body inside, crawling across the floor to where her mother's feet rested against the red plastic base of her chair. She lifted her timorous face up to the Matriarch and waited. The Matriarch looked into her daughter's gray, animal eyes. How had she endured it—the journey through the city, the crossing of the river, the emptiness of the forest? And how was it that she'd known which way was home? Her throat constricted. It seemed impossible that she could have ever thought to send her daughter away, that she could have actually sent her off with her brother, to be hauled through the woods in that rusty old wheelbarrow— what kind of mother had she become? It was the city, the great stone silence of the city: it had made her behave callously, forgetting what it was that she owed to them. No; it was the children, her heart insisted, who had shut her out. They spoke to one another in a language that neither she nor her brother understood, and even when she tried to imagine a way into their minds it was impossible for her to ascertain what it was that they really wanted, what they hoped for the future. Or was it that the world-as-it-was was simply enough for them—that they wanted nothing other than to fight and fuck beneath the hard white light of a sun she no longer recognized, until the poison in the air took the last of their breaths or tumors inevitable as time blocked up

their pale throats? Sorrow—a sadness as big as the universe—
burned at the corners of her eyes, but her brother was watching and she couldn't show that she was suffering in front of
him. It was impossible, how they lived. She thought of the
schoolmaster muttering in the dust. "If only some flood—"

Dolores reached forward and touched her mother's
foot; her fingers dug into the Matriarch's thick woolen sock,
and in this way she undid her mother, who pushed herself
up from her seat and stepped down from the electric wheelchair. The Matriarch knelt beside her abused daughter and
folded her in her arms and thought to herself—*Everybody
else is dead and I'm all alone!*—and outside a cloud scudded
across a sky that was as vast and as unforgiving as the desert
and nothing, nothing was forgiven.

If Only Someone Would Get Aquinas in *Here* (ii)

That night the Matriarch had a dream, not a vision, but a dream, and her dream went like this:

Television, thought Aquinas, was the only living art. Outside was dead and cold, but here, in the warm, pulsing interior of the screen, everyone and everything was quick with life, a squirming, exuberant life that once expressed ran from audience to performer and back to the audience again, guided or led by the gleaming white immensity of the eye. He'd heard it said before that all love was in the eye, and it was true that, surrounded by so many of them, Aquinas felt more loved than ever. But the sheep was watching him too, he knew it without having to turn around, could feel the ovine intensity of its gaze on the back of his neck. They stood in a carpeted depression bordered on three sides by the sloping ring of their audience, who had all paid money, real money, to be here. Up in the ring they cheered and whooped, although the show was still some five minutes away from starting. Aquinas let the warm wave of their expectation wash over him. He would have liked to attribute the popularity of the show to his personal charisma, but it was a fact that people loved *Get Aquinas in Here* because they loved problems. They wanted to be engrossed in them, to navigate the ins and outs of a thorny or difficult situation so thoroughly that at the end of the hour they could consider the experience a victory capable of making up for the miserable intractability of their own lives. In the history of the show there had never been a problem that Aquinas had left unsolved, and his fans felt strongly that the body of proof behind him was security against an uncertain future, so that for them there were no such things as unsolvable problems, but simply problems to which Aquinas had not yet been introduced. He had fans, armies of them. Enough to horrify the sheep, with their T-shirts and highlighter halos. What did they know about God or the sacred texts? For them Aquinas was only a collection of aphorisms and fatherly winks. And what the sheep knew was that this vaunted problem-solving ability was nothing more than the saintly wiles of someone who had been alive for over seven hundred years, who had been everywhere and seen almost everything. Inside the intimidating sweep of his monk's habit, Aquinas was small and cheerful. He smiled and revealed a set of perfectly white teeth. The sheep, hidden in the shadows behind the stage lights, watched Aquinas with something like contempt in its woolly heart. If the sheep could speak it would have told the audience that instead of digging away at the souls of others they ought to tend to their own. It sighed and crunched on an apple given to it by one of the lighting technicians. As though he was privy to the sheep's thoughts, Aquinas turned his head to look at it.

His eyes struggled with the movement from the bright light before him to the darkness behind him, and he became aware of the sheep in stages. Soon he was able to discern the position of its little black head even within the surrounding darkness due to the fact that the triangle of the sheep's face was surrounded by a halo of white wool, a fuzzy mane in which strands of light tangled, caught up in its crimps. What this meant was that despite everything the sheep was lit with a pale glow, a saintly light that reminded Aquinas for the umpteenth time that the sheep was superior to him in matters of the soul, because his own halo was a painter's imposition, history's trick, and Aquinas had long since succumbed to the temptation of celebrity. The sheep made him feel uncomfortable. He thought about the coded reprimand of its rectangle eyes, and all around him the audience murmured like the sea. They craned their heads forward, bulging on long rooster necks, and the yellow plastic chairs trembled with the weight of their bodies, the great American body that united them all, thought Aquinas, studying the mound of his own soft belly and the televisual neutrality of his chubby hand, which was a buzz of noise, semi-real, and piety took him as suddenly as fever: the green and purple whorls of the cheap carpet beneath him patterned Eden, let him know that God was everywhere. The famous theme started to play.

A woman in black wraparound sunglasses sat in an overstuffed armchair in the middle of the circle. Opposite her, an old man, as insubstantial as she was weighty, was almost lost inside another armchair. Aquinas walked toward them, and the audience watched the pair. They weren't convinced by

the woman and the sunglasses that hid her from them, or by
the way that she studied her short, dirty fingernails. They
were already aligned with the man; he was more sympa-
thetic. They could tell that she was on a high horse, looking
as if the pressure of the screen meant nothing to her. It was
also possible they liked him more than her because he was a
man and she was a woman and women are *liars*, and there
wasn't much Aquinas could do about that, but he wished
he'd taken the time to tell her to smile a little, to try to win
them over. Though maybe he hadn't said that because he
had known in advance how she would be: proud, unreason-
able. He rubbed his hands together and smiled. Then the
old man wriggled in his seat. His head flopped down, his
chin resting on his chest. Aquinas hurried to his side. "None
of that!" he said cheerfully, and took the man's bristly white
chin in his hand, tilting his face up to look at the audience.
They smiled and waved. "You old silly! You're here to tell us
what the matter is, not sleep!" The atmosphere in the room
was warm and encouraging. Aquinas hoped the old man
knew what they expected from him. He needed to moan,
groan, take his head in his hands, and win them over. He
needed to perform—just a little! He needed to tell them how
it had been, although of course no one could ever know
how it had been—the old man would tell his story and his
sister would counter him with a story of her own, and both
stories would belong to the world and its fury. But the show
was about truth because Aquinas knew how to find it, how
to sieve through the earthly dross and gather what remained,
which was cold, hard, objective fact, or so he liked to think.
He beamed at the audience and put his hand on the old

man's shoulder. "How can we know what the matter is if you won't say?" The audience agreed. The woman scowled. The old man tried to climb out of his seat but whenever he managed to lift himself up a little Aquinas pushed him back. When at last the old man began to speak the sound of his voice was the sound of rain falling on the bed of a dried-up creek. As his voice grew stronger, it carried them toward memories of a world that hadn't died and a cataclysm that never started. A white sun rolled over them. Aquinas closed his eyes.

***

When she'd first arrived in the city, she'd been all alone except for him, and it was he who had looked after her when she'd wept and screamed and thrown herself against the walls of the small bedroom that they shared, brother and sister. And though it was rumored that they shared a bed, this had not been true because in this city they shared nothing apart from the grim white fact of the room and her misery, which belonged to the past and was also their misery, a family misery, and as it would follow them wherever they went his sympathy was predicated on the simple understanding that if not her, him. But they were also joined by something beyond sadness, and when he reflected on it further it struck him that what pulled them together was nothing other than an immense vanity, because they were so similar, as if her face were the proof of his. Despite the fact that they were only siblings and not twins, it was true that even in the sprawl of their family people often forgot this distinction as a result of this incredible similarity of feature and gesture. They had been lumped together since birth, only a single year to separate them, and had grown up in unison, though she had always been in charge. All this had meant that when she had announced her intention to forsake their city for another it had only been natural that he'd follow her lead, being the younger and more docile of the pair. It had been essential for her to escape their fat-fingered mother (although even then he had known that it was inevitable she'd become a fat-fingered mother of her own) and in the first burst of their freedom she had been happy and unencumbered. Only before long the past drew even with her. The stemma of the family! The whole sick mess of it! He wasn't sure where to assign responsibility. It was clear that something was tormenting her, and as she tossed and turned on the white bed she gritted out that whatever it was was in her head, that a bright pink worm with their mother's face was there, deep inside her brain, chewing away and giving her no peace. It had wriggled in through her ear while she slept in her childhood bed on the tense, excited night before their departure for the city and the strange future it embodied, because the worm, too, had sensed the possibility of escape. It was this worm that ate away at her now, riddling her with loneliness and preventing her from catching the trick of it, the language of the new city, while her brother could already manage a few words, was already caught up in its strange and guttural rhythms, though he hid it, didn't want to admit that he was capable of leaving her behind. But he'd had his problems with the way she never called anything by its name and in doing so lost herself in a web of symbols that possessed only a glancing association with what was real and tangible, and so he couldn't do anything about the worm, and neither could he talk her back to the past and the world that had been theirs; and he thought it had something to do with language, with the fact that the language of the city was not their own and so she had had nothing to break the fall into the receptacle of herself, the miswired circuitry of her head, with its heaping, grasping associations. The worm! The wolves! The poison in the water! She was tired, exhausted by the drama of life in the alien city. She wanted to go back but didn't know how. Their family, the stink of failure— these things frightened her more than the timeless gray present into which she had slipped without knowing why. It hadn't been clear to him that they were different, that the similarity of their faces and their shared history did not, after all, mean everything, but once in the new city he understood, suddenly, that she was not him and he was not her. When he went to the university and started to study the distance between them grew. It was at the university that he had met his wife. His sister had been glad when the city died and even gladder when eleven years later his wife did too. She had taken their survival as a sign of something greater and his wife had been in the way of her mission. But the truth was that she had always been jealous of his wife, who belonged to the city and the new life that had never welcomed her the way she'd expected to be welcomed. She didn't want to make a place for her in her new image of the world. His wife's city—the city that his sister had come to hate—was dead. The abandoned skyscrapers were humbled at last. The parks with their shady paths would burn and one day the great river would dry up. His sister was new, alive, invigorated by the change. Until the discovery of the old schoolmaster, it had just been the three of them and she had been the one to find them food and shelter, to lead them through the contaminated areas and to force them to survive. She had pushed them to keep on living with the same mad ferocity that he had seen in her as a child, and she had hated his wife for her willingness to let it end. His wife had looked at the dead earth and seen nothing to redeem them. She was ashamed of the vanished animals, the poisoned rivers, and the barren fields. And even from the beginning of their relationship she had let him know that she was infertile. She hadn't cared—she had known long before the cataclysm that the city was going in a bad direction and the last thing she had wanted to do was to add to the misery she saw around her. His wife had never wanted to inflict the spectacle of the world on anyone else, but his sister wanted a baby. For them to be the last humans ever, eking it out in the ruins of the old city, waiting for death—his sister had hated the idea! She had pleaded with him; he hadn't given in. Eventually she had swallowed her pride and asked his wife. Until that moment he had never realized how strong her sense of purpose was. Her visioning—the ark, renewal, time's beginning again—had taken him unawares. Who could have guessed that she felt it so strongly, the future coiled up in her? But his wife had relented to his sister's desire for continuity, despite her own love of endings. She had seen her suffering and couldn't bear it. And so the very qualities he'd admired most about his wife were what pushed him into sleeping with his sister. It wasn't wrong, she had said to him, to want to make a go of it. If they couldn't find others, they could make them. Once he'd gotten over his initial disgust and admitted the attraction that had always been present in their too-closeness, sex with his sister acquired the kind of sick, solipsistic pleasure that he associated with masturbation. It wasn't wrong, his wife had said, to give her what she wanted, which she had the decency to pretend was only children and nothing to do with the taboo of his body; the desecration of the last remaining familial bond. The names of their surviving children were a prayer to life, an offering made to a god who he suspected was no longer there. Jan, Bara, Katka, Adela . . . It never stopped bothering him that she'd given them the names of the city, as if this were her final joke on it, and he'd never been won over by the project—which remained, sullenly, *her* project—just as how in the life before he had never been won over by children and the futurity they embodied because his wife's passivity was his own, and all he had wanted was to let the world drift past him. After the conquest of her brother and his wife, his sister had flourished. She grew bigger and stronger, while it seemed to him that his own wife weakened, as if the life his sister was brimming with had been siphoned off her. The significance of their survival, the idea that there had to be a reason behind their solitary existence in the empty world, sustained her, gave her strength. Even the later appearance of the fat schoolmaster did nothing to dent her faith. The cataclysm had confirmed everything that his sister believed about their world. In time he came to understand that the expression he'd caught on her face when the three of them had emerged from the faculty basement and encountered the deserted streets, the silent city, and the blasted countryside, had, if anything, been *gloating*, as if now that reality mirrored what had always been her idea of it, she could finally let go of her sadness and be free. But everything that he had loved was dead. His sister's sadness, *their* sadness, had leapt from her heart to his, and the burden of life weighed him down like a rock. His sister could make the world in her image and there was nothing to stop her. He didn't care, couldn't care. Someday he would end it, but it had always been hard to end things, and now their uncle saw that it was harder than ever. He put his head in his hands and wailed. The Matriarch gave no sign that she had heard him. The lights went out, the spectators sighed, and then nothing was heard save for the quiet, regular breathing of the little white sheep, a pale glimmer in the void. The audience waited.

***

By the end of the month the Matriarch was ready with her story, the same story as usual. It had pleased her that the weeks following the return of Dolores had been hot and dry, too heavy for change, though at all times she had been aware of the children and their waiting. Nothing had come from the forest and the Matriarch had understood at last that the threat came from those closest to her. She sat in her chair on the concrete platform above the square and the children massed below. They gathered around their mother not because they loved her but because her body was a net that stretched out over their world and caught up everything they knew.

"In the years after the flood there was nothing but silence," she began, "and the city and the forest were covered by an inland sea, a limitless stretch of dark water in which no individual form could be discerned." Her mother's voice scratched across the surface that was Agathe, again, a disk, that spread blackly along a flat white canvas. It was in this shape—a sulk of tar—that Agathe lurked and listened to the scalpel of sound emitted from the hard pink line of her mother's lips, while their uncle, a faint speckling of brown dots, crouched mistily at the Matriarch's feet. Her mother cleared her throat and something convulsed in the sunny attic room of Agathe's mind: she observed a rippling of surfaces. "Everything was the same. Nothing was distinct. It was an invasion—" That old story. Had it really been so terrible? Her speech spun out into the dusk, a scrape of wool. Agathe, a girl again, placed her head in her hands and looked up at her mother. Above them the sky was feverish. And because the whole camp was there, congregated beneath her, the Matriarch tried again, "It was an *invasion*—"

She dabbed at the surface of her sunglasses with the dirty fabric of her sleeve, and Agathe could see that the Matriarch was thinking about a city that spread across the surface of the world, whose vegetal roads unfurled into the surrounding darkness in ever-widening intestinal loops because, she whispered to herself, the story of the city was always a story of disintegration. What their mother had hated about their city was that it had already been on the edge, halfway to collapse, and so it was the case that this future had been encoded in it all along, in the dark metal skyscrapers of the business districts, in the wailing outskirts with their pitiful housing projects, in the deathly silence of the orderly suburbs . . . everything winding down, declining, until the world was one great and devout listening, holy because it required nothing and no longer dreamed of any future; if objects, having spoken their truths, dared to shut up. The Matriarch would do anything to confound this kind of silence. Now her voice was desperate, ". . . there was nothing *holy* about it . . ." and their uncle rocked fitfully beside Agathe. She watched as he placed his thin arms around the hump of his knees and buttoned himself up against them; his strange, secret thoughts began to clang around in the cauldron of his head. Next, she looked over at Jakub, where he stood with Marta at the fringes of the semicircle that surrounded the Matriarch. Marta whispered something in his ear and a moment later Jakub laughed, but his yelp was lost within a general murmuring that made it clear that nobody cared about the Matriarch's story, that it was only habit and the cumulative weight of the years that kept them sitting there with their faces tilted up to observe her, hearing without listening, so that when her sentences reached the children they did so only as discrete sounds, without narrative or conviction. They watched their mother with vacant, murderous smiles, and she was nervous. Even Jan was hardly listening to her. He stood at the edge of the crowd, surrounded by his sisters, who were using their stolid bodies to shield him, because the Matriarch had taken a dim view of his treatment of Dolores, which had been another unforeseen event, another sign. After what had happened to her, their sister had wept and moaned in her sleep, gurgling her misery to the indifferent concrete surface of the ceiling, but Agathe had felt no pity for her, nothing except a cool scientific interest in how the proceedings had taken place, and she'd laughed along with the others because Dolores had got what was coming to her. "Dolores had got what was coming to her." It even sounded like a phrase Jan would use, wrapped up as he was in what their uncle described as "an endless play of slights, insults, grudges, and requitals," and it was a statement that removed their fat, ineffectual sister from the realm of their pity (if it existed), confirmed her wet, lonely sobbing, and said: *Don't worry, there's more to come.* Agathe slunk a glance to where Dolores sat with Jan's children on the other side of the circle. The sun dipped below the dark green line of the trees and a plume of orange light curved along the horizon. Every year they moved further away from a hopelessly dissolute past and a rotten old language whose referents had thankfully *vanished*, but it seemed to Agathe that the language they used now knew only violence, the pain and squalor of the present there in their jagged sentences, words like expulsions of breath, the same dull repetition of formulae—"A *flood* of light across the gray waters"—yes, she was thinking with her uncle's head because Agathe didn't care about beauty, and as she watched the dome of his skull became the sphere of the amalgamate earth. The Matriarch stood still in her greenhouse of words. She looked at Jakub and he looked back at her, his face half-hidden behind the curve of Marta's cheek, which reflected the dying light as a brutal gleam. "It is impossible to imagine a reality that does not believe in progress," she said, frowning a little. "The continued success of our enterprise—our purpose cannot be questioned." But even as she said this, they were questioning her, Dolores stuck out like a great white thumb within the crowd of children. Someone began to laugh. The Matriarch couldn't believe it, how much ground she had already lost, and so without stopping to consider the consequences she began to tell them a different story, a new story.

"On the other side of the city there is another forest," the Matriarch said, and the children, surprised, fell silent. "In the old world we went there, back when he still studied at the university in the theology department." She pointed to their uncle, but the children continued to look at her. "We took the train to Beroun, he bought our tickets, I couldn't speak the language. We walked up the hill through the forest and the sun broke through the canopy and everything beneath it was brilliant with light. We were all alone, your aunt had stayed in the city, and for the first time since we had moved there I felt happy, as if it wasn't so hard after all: life, their language." The Matriarch removed her sunglasses and granted them the sight of her eyes, which were gray like theirs. "When we reached the top of the hill, we saw it, an old fortress, but at first all my attention was absorbed by one tall tower and I thought that what I was seeing was a light-house, though of course there was no water for hundreds of miles. My whole life I was afraid of water. When the world died I saw the sea race inward, it swallowed everything up, only nobody else could see it—the water was everywhere but somehow invisible, and I told the others that it wasn't the light that had destroyed the city but a *flood*—" The children looked at one another with veiled expressions. "Not light, but water, everything mixing together, the silence was intolerable—" Their uncle interrupted, "She dreamed of a ship, this felt significant," and instead of reprimanding him the Matriarch straightened up in her seat. "A ship—I dreamed of a ship—"

But the Matriarch couldn't say what it was that she had known. The silence screeched across the square. Before long the children began to giggle. What had she expected? It was too late to alter the fabric of their relationship, to cut a new pattern. The children hadn't understood her. They stared at the crumpled figure in the electric wheelchair and wondered where their mother had gone. Was it a test? Was she punishing them? It was too much; her authority dripped away. The Matriarch was beginning to sense the enormity of her error. She reached for the old ending, but she couldn't even find that, and after a fearful look at the assembled children she was off with a sputtering of the wheelchair's motor. They couldn't bear to look at her go, so they looked at the ground instead. The last slivers of light retreated.

Their circle was broken. The children dispersed, giggling. Sounds—the rattling of the door as their mother disappeared back into her office, the muttered pacts between siblings—were absorbed into the changing sky, scattered with dark clouds. Their uncle leaned against the edge of the concrete platform and began to fall asleep; Agathe, still crouched beside him, watched as a small group formed around Marta and Jakub by the dormitory wall. She decided that Jakub had positioned himself in this way because he wanted to be heard: he wanted the Matriarch to hear every single one of his words because he was using them against her; yes—Agathe thought, moving closer to where they knelt in the dry grass—he was really dragging her through the mud, and she couldn't defend herself from her office, across the wall that she'd built between herself and them. Now Jakub exploited her absence, and the Matriarch's story was roundly subjected to derision. Marta quaked with laughter, her hands over her mouth. The others—Adam, Marek, and Mary, Jakub's particular friends—grinned. Agathe hesitated at the edge of their circle, wanting neither to be noticed nor forgotten. Across the square a fire was being lit and the younger children were chattering around it, Jan puffing away with his leathery cheeks billowing in and out like the bellows in a smithy. He threw a disgruntled glance in their direction. Jakub had been speaking as loudly as he could, but when he caught Jan looking at him he dropped his voice to a whisper. "There aren't any others, everything is the same as always, but she couldn't stand it any longer. The purpose—what purpose? She wants us to stay the same, to do whatever she wants without complaining." Marek agreed. "It's all the same, she only talks about herself, thinks about herself." The moon swam into the sky and Mary looked up at it. "It's because we're all alone." "It wouldn't matter if there were more of them, people like us," Jakub replied. "We would still be alone because they would be just like us—they don't know what's going on or what happened to the others, all the people who lived before. Who cares if Dolores saw them, and I don't think she *did*—" "Dolores cares—" Adam said. "Why don't you ask her what the other humans look like? She'll be able to give you details—*physical* details . . ." The others were laughing again, but Jakub kept on talking. "She's *insane*, completely *insane*— she went mad with the rest of them. She doesn't have a clear

image of how things should be, there's no plan . . ." he continued, and Marta interrupted him, suddenly earnest: "The
others *will* come, Jan says. Because of Dolores—they'll
come here and kill us all because she betrayed them." Jakub
lost his temper. "There aren't any others!" Marta ignored
him and looked across their circle at Adam. She said, "Or
maybe they got rid of her because they didn't want her, she
wasn't good enough." "You'd have to ask Dolores," Adam replied, and Marta snorted. "I wouldn't want to ask Dolores
about anything"—"Imagine fucking her"—"Jan already did
that"—another explosion of laughter. Agathe squeezed in
beside Marta. She put her head in her sister's lap and Marta
tangled her fingers in Agathe's dirty black hair. On her other
side Mary paid her no notice, but Adam leaned forward and
smiled. "Look—an idiot has come to join us." Agathe said,
"I'm not an idiot." Marta brushed the hair away from her
forehead and crooned, "You are, you are." Agathe made a
face and squirmed in her lap. "Be still," Marta told her. "Stay
here with me for a while." She dipped her head down and
kissed Agathe just above her ear. "You're my daughter—my
little daughter." "I'm not," said Agathe. Adam picked up her
foot in his hands and examined it without saying anything.
He looked back at Agathe and when he spoke again his tone
was pleasant. "Why do you think we all ignore you?" Marta
began to pull Agathe's hair back from her face. "It's her head
that's broken, of course she won't answer you." They were
both giggling, Marta covering Agathe's eyes with her hands
and Adam pulling her toward him with one hand wrapped
around her ankle and the other starting to slip beneath her
skirt. "Leave her alone," said Jakub, and Adam moved away.

Marta caught Agathe smiling and flicked her ear. "Don't get too excited, moron." Jakub addressed the circle again. "We could change things. We could make things better. We don't need to find others." Mary looked at the ground. "Brothers and sisters aren't meant to fuck." "But they do anyway," Marta said with a big smile.

It's hopeless, Jakub thought, and despair rolled over him. At night he dreamed of a presence, a solitary white-haired scientist who had survived the cataclysm and waited for him in one of the abandoned tower blocks at the city center; he was waiting for Jakub with both of his hands laid flat on a cool metal table, and when Jakub got there he would explain everything, lay out the history of the world and the disaster in calm objective terms and perhaps even proffer a solution, tell the blond-haired boy what it was necessary to do to escape his family and what the schoolmaster called "that nest of sin," the mud, the light, the field, the endless, pointless lessons . . . Now his mind was the screech of the schoolmaster's fingernail against the blackboard when he wanted to startle the class, cut through the lethargy of the light—their minds cracked, riddled with holes, but still capable of being brought to the edge, coherent in that moment, the necessary pain—ah yes, he'd had enough of it, it was in him too, and that was why his head hurt so much. He looked at Agathe with hatred in his pale eyes because she belonged to the new world, the tumbledown second-rate reality that was their sentence for the sins of their ancestors: the old factories whirring without stopping, black smoke churning across the sky; ice tumbling into dark green waters already bereft of life; the seething, copulating virus of humanity, refusing to stop, even in the face of the coming disaster, and perhaps even fucking more furiously *because of it.* The clinging—it was the way that they clung to it that appalled him—the incessant clinging to life and the destruction of everything else until they were alone, utterly alone, on the dead black ball of the world, their cities, empires, and nations disappeared. *If it was so bad,* Agathe's face asked him, *then why do you want to go back?* Jakub couldn't answer her. This world was hers, not his—he didn't know what he wanted, but he did know that he didn't want anything from Agathe.

"Maybe we should kill her," said Marta. "Our mother?" asked Marek. Mary giggled. "It won't happen." "Why not?" said Adam. Marta's fingers carried on raking through Agathe's hair. She could feel the warmth of her sister's thigh on the back of her scalp and wondered what it would be like to be enveloped by her, just like Jakub. She began to imagine Dolores with Jan, feeling, for one moment, the blunt force of his boot as it drove into her own side. Was there something that she shared with Dolores? A sympathy of blows, the gift of a kick, or was the pain of the boot a ghost pain, not real at all, some kind of sister-feeling between them that said, *Yes, we're all human here*? She grimaced; the sensation left her. It was so hard to stay in one place. Marta stroked her hair and Agathe smiled at Adam. He picked up her foot again and dug his fingernails into the rough skin of its sole, but she didn't move at all. The night was full of sorrow. She could hear the crackling of the flames and the sighing of their uncle as he slithered across the square, the ground scraping against his worn suit jacket, stiff with the dust of the century that he had left behind. He had crawled out of the wreckage of their world, and over the years the jacket had turned the wearied gray that they associated with their uncle. He was close enough to them now that Agathe could smell him, and when she turned her head to look in their uncle's direction the weak orange light from Jan's fire revealed a portion of his ponderous face, the broken glasses sliding to the tip of his long nose and his thin lips twitching as if he were having an endless and tiresome conversation with himself.

"Why are you crawling?" Jakub asked, and those cracked disks angled toward them. "I don't know," their uncle replied. "You were thinking about her story," Marta said accusingly. "You were crawling along and thinking about her story, I can read your mind like the back of my hand." Their uncle dug his elbows into the earth and raised his head up. Marta repeated herself, "I know you—I can read your mind," and then their uncle nodded. "Unwise—it was terribly unwise to talk about the past. It's our secret; you were never part of it. Reason, cities of reason, a shared purpose that spanned continents. Everything in place and accounted for. It wasn't so bad. Now there is neither faith nor reason; the system is dead, vanished, for all that she keeps on trying to build her own. Yes, it was terribly unwise of her to start talking about the past, the real past. What good did she think it would do? You're all animals." They looked at him with their identical eyes, and their uncle blinked. "I didn't want to talk to you." "Well, you've started now," Marta said, but their uncle was already crawling away, the back of his balding head reflecting the weak, stuttering light of Jan's fire. Adam bent down and put Agathe's toe in his mouth. She looked at his bowed head and thought that her brother was a collection of parts, each with a unique mechanical purpose—though her sisters were as fluid and indivisible as the curves of the schoolmaster's beloved sculptures, her brother was a composite, a mass of predetermined functions, hydraulics, hinges, bolts—and watching him she thought that there was something awful and ugly about that fixed complexity; he could never be any other way. Agathe was thrilling from the attention, but as Adam curled his tongue around her toe her foot jerked away of its own accord. Marta leaned over and slapped Adam. "Leave her alone!" she said cheerfully. Their brother stood up and put his boot on Agathe's stomach. "If I stamped down you'd be dead." Agathe stuck out her tongue and Marta answered for her. "You kill my little baby and our mother will find out and kill *you*." "She wouldn't."—"She would!" He spat something out that they couldn't hear before walking away from the group. Then Mary put her hand on Marek's shoulder and the two of them disappeared into the shadows behind the schoolroom. Jakub followed them, and now Agathe and Marta were alone, without even the accompaniment of Jan's soft cursing, the group by the fire having long since dispersed. The darkness pressed in on them, and Marta said, "Don't worry—once the light from the fire is gone we'll be able to see in the dark—it will be a different kind of dark." She continued to stroke Agathe's hair. "Today you're my daughter and I'm your mother. I've always wanted a baby of my own." Agathe said nothing. "You wouldn't know much about it because you're a moron, but only a few of us can have them—maybe—and the rest of us can't. It's the poison—it's in the trees, the earth, the water—everywhere. Our uncle told me and our sisters did too. It's in me and you."

From the vantage point of the moon the earth was green, growing, changing, and maybe even thriving; as it moved away from their history of smoke and metal it became stronger, remembered its own past, how the world had been before them. A star loped into the sky, and Marta's voice was buried beneath something that nobody but Agathe could hear, the murmuring of *life*: there, behind everything else, were other voices too, things that were just beginning, although the sky had changed color when the old world died and the rivers of the earth were rivers of poison and the soil gray—*It isn't over yet!* they were saying to her and she was beaming their message back up to them with a strange and savage joy. The planet would survive, and she would survive because she belonged to the light. Agathe said, "What's it like with Jakub?" Marta looked down at her. "It's just like it is with everyone else. It's fun. Not boring. Haven't you done it with anyone yet?" The pale corona of her hair reflected the white worm-trail of the moon as it slid across the sky, not so pure now; the whole thing in motion, spinning, always—*It will never stop*, said the fat white eye of the moon, looking down at them. "It's easy, once you know how. If you have a baby we can share." Agathe grimaced. A shuffling sound from somewhere near the edge of the square caught her attention. She narrowed her eyes and stared into the shadows that pooled beneath the entrance of the schoolroom, but Marta said it before she could. "It's Dolores."

Agathe pulled herself up into a sitting position. "No— she sleeps when it goes dark." Marta said, "She can't sleep." "Why?" Agathe asked, and Marta continued, "I heard her yesterday and the day before too." *It's warm, she can't sleep because it's too warm*, thought Agathe. She concentrated on the darkness in front of her and made out the shape of their sister, a white moonish lump surrounded by shadow—Dolores, the moon: the white, hulking mass of her sister's lumpy body was a crude and lumpy metaphor, and the moon was a traitor, too, a sly and sickly half-wit—it had never revealed the true shape of things. Then Dolores—the real Dolores—slopped out of the shadows with her back humped up like a camel's. The moon lapped at her sister's round face with its tongue of light, and Agathe could see that her mouth was moving without stopping, trembling all over like a stone does before an avalanche, only here the crisis would never arrive: she'd never find the words, existing, as she did, in the space between vegetable activity and human speech; now her mouth made an O—her big loose lips made a wide O that was language's ghost, taut with effort, and then the shape was lost again to the inarticulate, wordless quivering of her mouth, the baby's blubbering, her face scrunched up with effort. Marta said, "If you open your mouth like that someone will stuff something into it." Her sentence cut across the square to Dolores, sailing down her ear canal all the way to the webby matter of her brain, where Marta's words were scrambled and rearranged and nothing was understood. Dolores gave no sign that she had heard her sister and went on with her silent lamenting, her unfocused eyes staring off into the distance. Marta tucked her legs beneath her and inched forward until she sat on the same invisible line as Agathe. "She can't sleep because she's going to have a baby." Agathe said, "No." Marta smiled. "She is. I know it. It isn't fair, but she is."

Agathe looked at Dolores. Now her head lay sideways, face tilted up to the sky and her mouth incessantly forming the syllables of her own secret proto-language. The lower half of her body—the stumpy mermaid's tail of her abbreviated legs—remained buried in the shadows and so Dolores was cut in half by the light: only her torso lay there in the grass, supported by her flabby arms and the enormous breasts: she was a throwaway, a discarded experiment; the slip of the potter's wheel or the sculptor's hands. "She's too dumb!" "It only takes a hole," Marta said, watching their sister mumble in the dirt. Agathe couldn't speak. The white moon crushed into them. Marta reached over and brushed her hand against her younger sister's shoulder. Agathe wanted to say something to her but was halfway out of her head already; Dolores had stolen her tongue—or maybe she'd never had the words anyway, the right words, to say what she meant—and so instead she placed her head on the ground too. Marta leaned above her again. "My daughter—my little daughter." A wet kiss on the back of her skull, her matted dark hair. A cry rang out— somewhere in the distance, from one of the buildings on the other side of the square—swelled up, and was finished off by the soft thud of a kick; a thin wailing scrolled into the night— said what she couldn't—and Dolores moaned and stuck her thick fingers in her ears.

***

The first thing that Agathe knew was that Mary was shaking her. "Wake up! Wake up!" She looked up at her sister with confusion in her eyes. The sun chinked in through the shuttered dormitory windows—she realized that she was lying in bed. "Everybody else has gone and I'm all alone," Mary said, and when Agathe tried to roll away, her older sister hauled her upright and began to drag her toward the dormitory door. Outside the sky was an even, featureless blue, the sun so bright that it was painful to look at anything; the dull gray of their mother's apartment block gleamed agonizing silver, while the tan buildings scattered near the wall were transformed into quadrangles of light. They stumbled along the edge of the square with squinting, watery eyes. Beneath them the mud had been castellated by sun and wind, tossed up into sharp turrets that cut through the thin soles of their boots and drew the occasional wince or muffled curse. When they reached the low building that served as the children's canteen, halfway down the path that led to the apartment block where Jan lived with his sisters and their children, both of them were panting. Inside everything had been cleared away; there was nothing left except a few dirty dishes and crumbs. At the farthest end of the room, past the long metal tables and disorder of chairs, lurked an oblong of green shadow. They stood together in the middle of the room and wondered what to do next. There was no noise from outside, not even the shrieking of the younger children floating over from Jan's building. The canteen stank of rotting food. Agathe took a few steps toward the door as if she wanted to make a run for the dormitory, but Mary grabbed her wrist. "No, today you have to keep me company, everybody else is gone. That's what you wanted, wasn't it? Company. Well, now's your chance. You can spend some time with me." Her straw hair was lit up by the yellow light that poured in from the open door behind them. She dragged her younger sister outside again and pointed to where the Matriarch's apartment block loomed on the other side of the square. "We'll go upstairs. We can sit in one of the upper rooms and look down at the camp." Agathe nodded, suddenly indifferent, and together they clambered up the path to their mother's building. The whole time Mary was looking around without much hope. The encampment was deserted—had her siblings left on a trip through the forest to one of the old shopping centers? Undoubtedly Jan had sent them—who else could coax an effort from that reluctant, surly cohort?—though he, too, was nowhere to be seen, and Mary wished she was with them in the forest, where it would be cooler, the light broken up by the canopy into sheets of dimming sky, and she would not be alone with Agathe in the tomb of the camp, caught in this leaden dialogue between sun and earth. If only she had woken up in time! It was so warm that every step felt like an effort, and she couldn't stop thinking about their mother's story and the night that had followed. She had liked being with Marek, who was slow and calm and of all her brothers the most like her, but later when Franta had climbed over her in the stifling dormitory, repulsion had struggled with lethargy, and lethargy had won. As the others drifted off to sleep, Mary had become aware that she wasn't really there, that all that was in her bed was a lump of toppled flesh, already defeated, and being so defeated could it really be said that lethargy was the reason for her surrender? The sun and the schoolroom had wiped her away, whatever it was that she had won for herself, and so she had watched her brother violate her body from a high corner, up on the ceiling with the spiders and their webs. If only she could be more like Marta! If only she could wallow in it. The light, the forest, the field. Something always jabbing into her, another brother, and her big, tired body too stunned to help it. They sawed away at her under the aegis of life. But Mary hadn't believed the things the Matriarch had said about their glorious future, and nor had she taken the sending-away of their younger sister as anything other than a desperate act. She had watched Agathe and Dolores and had drawn her own conclusions. It was clear they couldn't go on in the way that they had started. If there were more children they would be like Jan's. The forest— which was empty, empty, despite what they said—crawled into her head. A great black welter of expectations hung over them all. *If only it would rain!* she thought, a curl of sweat in the hollow of her back. If only she could see into the knot of the past and walk into it too! When would her siblings be back? There was no telling. She looked at Agathe, struggling up the slope behind her, and felt it again, a deadly weariness.

When they reached their mother's building and peered into her office they found the Matriarch hunched up in the darkness alone, watching an episode of *Get Aquinas in Here*. They pressed their faces against the glass of the window and studied their mother through the gaps in the blinds, the sun whipping the backs of their heads. The television screen was a distant glowing square, but they had no problem making out the desolate brown field and the little figure of the farmer kneeling in the dry earth. Above him the vaulted sky stretched out, stony, impassive. The rain wouldn't come! The crops wouldn't grow! The dogs had eaten his chickens!

From somewhere in the distance they could hear them baying. The Matriarch watched the screen without blinking as the farmer lamented, but on the other side of the window Mary was rolling her eyes. As the camera zoomed in on the farmer's leathery face, streaked with rivulets of tears, she pulled Agathe away from the window and past the door to the Matriarch's office, leaving their mother alone with the farmer and his barren field. They made for the concrete overhang on the eastern side of the building where, their uncle had told them, ambulances had once idled between emergencies. It was cooler there, though the sun dashed white streaks between the columns. They leaned against the stucco wall and Mary examined Agathe again. Her dark hair fell over her face in strands—she was so stupid and sly that their older sisters never thought to take care of her. Had she been troubled by their mother's loss of control? Did it bother her that the encampment was on the edge of some great upheaval? Mary wasn't sure when she had begun thinking like this, but the idea hung in her mind like a terrible iron weight. Her sister's dark eyes were impassive. Mary decided to test her. "She's worried. That's why she's alone, thinking. She's losing her thread, she doesn't know what to do next." She paused and assembled the story in her mind before continuing in the same low voice. "The others won't come—there aren't any others—but everything we have here will be ruined because the boys won't tolerate her now that she's weak." She looked down at her damp hands. "And you don't want to imagine what it will be like if Jan is in charge." Agathe didn't answer her, and Mary realized that the only person she was scaring was herself. Hunched up in front of the television screen, the

Matriarch had struck her as unbearably frail. Her daughter
saw that fabled drive dwindling, life as they knew it grinding
to a halt, and unease washed over her; a light, cloudy anxiety.
She tried to remind herself that she'd known all along it
couldn't last from listening to what her older sisters had said
in the schoolroom before Jan began to lock them away one
by one, as they repeated the words their uncle's dead wife
had passed down to them, and then later from their woeful
reports in the field, but this was no comfort to her because
knowing was painful. She tugged Agathe toward the metal
door that opened onto the circular stairwell leading to the
upper levels of the apartment block. Inside the heat was ex-
hausting. Soon Mary's face was shiny with sweat from the
effort of climbing up the concrete steps. Agathe was already drifting. She wanted to go back to sleep, and when
they reached the long rectangular room on the sixth floor
that seemed to be their destination and Mary let go of her
hand, she flopped down onto the rotting wooden floor without a second thought. Her sister followed her down. "No,
no, don't go to sleep. I don't want to be by myself. I'll tell you
one of the stories, the old stories." Mary thought about it.
"I'll do the episode with the cheerleader and her brother; I'll
do it the way our sisters showed me." Agathe didn't sit up but
she didn't close her eyes either. She stared at the yellowing
ceiling and Mary began to speak in the voice of the anony-
mous Czech commentator, repeating his words in the same
bright, nihilistic tone.

   "It goes like this: there's a girl who grows up in a rich
family and has a charmed life. She's one of those beautiful
girls who just sails through adolescence: she experiences no

self-loathing, is comfortable in her own body, doesn't have to get braces, doesn't put on weight, sweat, get acne, anything. All of her friends undergo the trauma of puberty to some degree or another, but she's the kind of girl who when she gets her first period already has an organic cotton tampon inserted in her vagina because something in her genes— something in those perfect little helixes of DNA—lets her know in advance what will happen, and so she's not even a little discomfited or embarrassed when it does, but simply goes up to her equally beautiful and composed blond mother and says, 'Mom, I've started menstruating,' and that's that—no shame, no suffering, and probably not even any real blood. And this girl isn't just beautiful, but smart to boot, and so she easily negotiates her way through high school, and when she walks by in the corridors the teachers whisper among themselves and say things like 'Harvard,' and 'Princeton,' and ask themselves how somebody with such perfect skin can also have such a perfect mind; her pores are so small that her complexion is positively *matte*, and she's already read *The Critique of Pure Reason*, and, what's more, understood it too. Her teachers plan great things for her, and she simply tosses her blond hair and accepts that this is the way things are, though she tempers her fortune with the requisite humility, and importantly this isn't calculated at all—she's so kind and so nice that she genuinely wants to do everything she can to avoid making other people feel insecure. I'll reiterate that this isn't motivated by self-interest—by which I mean that very fortunate people often deliberately show their weaknesses and flaws in order to make life easier for themselves, as they want to be accepted and don't want others to dislike them—but because this girl has a real Christ-like interest in the well-being of other people, and even if she doesn't know why it is that she's been so happy and so blessed with her wealthy family, beautiful face, perfect skin, and ferocious intellect, she does know that she doesn't want the facts to hurt others, and so, despite and not because of all these gifts, the girl is popular, accepted, and loved; everyone wants her to come to their parties and nobody has a bad thing to say about her, even when the professors praise her in front of everybody else in the classroom and mutter things like 'Harvard' and 'Princeton' loud enough that the others can hear them too, because the embarrassed and humble smile that plays across her beautiful lips when the girl hears them say these things is enough to dissolve any jealousy or resentment in that very same moment. Therefore her adolescence passes without problems, not a single hint of unhappiness or ghost of doubt, and when high school graduation comes around our girl is declared valedictorian of the graduating class, and she makes a speech about how she won't forget any of them, how they will have a place in her heart for all eternity, even though she's moving away—*that's right, she's going to Harvard!*—because she knows that they all have incredible futures too, and besides, you never forget a true friend, and her speech is just the right mix of polished and sincere that everyone is crying, literally weeping in their seats, even the parents of other teenagers, and, of course, the teachers who have been muttering after her blond resplendence all these years; everyone is extremely touched, and her own parents are in floods of pride, but it's at this moment, at the height of her adolescent glory, that her dark-haired younger brother, only sixteen years old, has a massive epileptic seizure and falls to the floor and hits his head on the edge of the seat in front of him with a dull *thwack*. The sound echoes across the room, which is suddenly silent, and the large soccer mom in the aforementioned seat turns around and lows like a cow at twilight, and a moment later their own parents start screaming, shoving through the tidy rows of chairs in order to make their way to her brother, who by now is spasming on the floor and foaming at the mouth, and a thin rivulet of bright red blood runs from the place where his head made contact with the hard edge of the seat in front of him. They take him to the hospital in an ambulance that gets stuck in traffic, the West Coast traffic that can't be argued with, all clogged-up arterial roads—her high school graduation ceremony cut short, the first unexpected or bad thing that has happened so far in her charmed life—and when they finally make it there a small doctor with a clearly discernible paunch walks up to her parents and begins to talk, and as they nod and pay attention, the girl can't stop looking at the paunch through the clinical white fabric of his uniform, and it makes her think of compromise, ethical compromise, his sagging flesh a visual representation of how our will surrenders to the world, because even in the context of this hospital she can't stop thinking the very thoughts that make people say things like 'Harvard' and 'Princeton' when she walks by, but eventually the little doctor says with a reassuring smile that they have nothing to worry about, her brother will be okay, he has epilepsy, that's all, and millions of people all over the world have this condition and live perfectly ordinary, happy lives, so really, they should all be glad that it isn't something much more serious; while he says all this, his reassuring smile is tempered by a hint of droll humor, and it's a fact that they, as a family group, *are* reassured, and so after a week of inpatient monitoring they are allowed to take the younger brother home with a neat stack of boxes containing his new anti-epileptic drugs in the back of the car. With time they push the disaster of the high school graduation ceremony from their calm, blond minds and get back on with their lives: the girl goes away to Harvard, the father returns to his successful and demanding job, the mother gets her weekly facial, and the younger brother dutifully takes his medication every day and waits for his seizures to stop. But his seizures don't stop, and although he waits and tries to be patient, the younger brother starts to feel as if something in his mind has shifted in the chaos and the confusion, that he isn't the same as he was before, can't make sense of his thoughts, that kind of thing; his memory is in shambles: time—times—interlace in his mind and every thought is the hazy metaphor of another, every image a substitution; all this is to say that everything suggests everything else, and besides, his mind is full of holes because the younger brother is still having seizures *several times a day* and even the spaces between the events themselves are blurred and dreamy, his experience an endless drift of associations and links from which he can't unentangle himself no matter how hard he tries. As this goes on the younger brother starts to fail at school and lose friends—he can't remember why he had them and so he doesn't bother—and then something even worse happens, and it's this: His poor confused mess of a mind starts to center around the figure of his sister, his perfect blond sister, and even though the whole of their lives together they've treated each other with the mutual love and respect of which well-adjusted siblings are capable, and he's always received the news of her innumerable achievements with happiness and family pride, even though she's always been kind to him and now that he's sick calls him up every couple of days to ask him how he's doing, taking the time out of her thrilling and absorbing life on the East Coast to check on her poor little brother who is so clearly going through a difficult time, the younger brother starts to feel resentful toward his older sister, jealous of her life and the way everyone back home asks him about her as if she's some kind of fucking demigod. Soon enough he begins to fixate on his sister, and he even starts to think that his accident was her fault, that something in her speech set him off that day and what happened might have been avoided, the sequence never started, if she'd just *kept quiet*, or hadn't been in a position where she'd been expected to give a speech in the first place, which is to say, never striven after fame and glory, because this kind of striving has consequences, human consequences, and then he can barely hide the anger in his voice when they talk on the phone, and later at night as the younger brother lies in bed he thinks about her perfect skin and long legs and big eyes, and fumes—he can't stop thinking about his sister and how much he hates her for being so fucking perfect—and then comes the day when he's home alone—his parents are out at some function, and he doesn't have any friends left—and he's feeling *so* angry and *so* bitter and is just pacing around the house in a confused epileptic haze and he sees the photo of her that his parents keep on the mantel above the fireplace in which she is wearing her cheerleading outfit and smiling at the camera, and without really thinking about it he reaches into his pants and begins to jerk off while he swears at the photo, looking into her big blue eyes and telling her how much he hates her, blames her for everything—everything, literally everything, is her fault—and then when he ejaculates it's the best thing ever, better than any other time in his life, and from that moment onward it's not understating the matter to say that the younger brother becomes well and truly obsessed with his older sister, and by that I mean *sexually obsessed*: he hoards photographs of her and masturbates alone in his room, squawks out her name as he comes, doesn't even attempt to hide it from their parents, who, understandably, are shocked, utterly shocked; and when she calls him from college he lowers his voice to a whisper and tells her all the things that he's done to her in his mind, and she starts crying and asking him why and then he says raggedly that he's jerking off right now, can't she hear him, the *thwack thwack thwack* of his hand against his dick, and she hangs up with a heartbroken bleep. Their parents don't know what to do—who would?— and though they attempt to manage him in different ways, nothing sticks: the younger brother drops out of school, falls in with the wrong crowd, begins drinking and taking drugs, which of course makes his seizures *worse*, much worse, and his poor mind even more deranged, and then he uses the money that he inherited from their grandmother to move away from home where there is even less of a possibility of somebody being able to curtail his obscene and destructive behavior, and the whole time he keeps on sending his sister threatening and sexually explicit messages. Eventually, in a way, the family begins to adjust to this new and horrifying dynamic: with the younger brother no longer in the picture, their father starts to go golfing with a younger colleague, in addition to which he adopts a whole host of new habits and hobbies, while their mother begins to see a psychoanalyst and encouragingly signs up for an adult learning course in exactly the same field; meanwhile, the older sister does her best to stop thinking about her younger brother and get on with her life at college, where predictably she's doing amazingly, studying philosophy, mathematics, and computer science, and already being courted for a graduate program at MIT; in addition to which she's met a beautiful and perfect guy called Brad and he's even proposed to her, the idea being that they'll get married straight after graduation, and so the letters and calls from her younger brother are really the only fly in her ointment, albeit a fly of no mean size, but she changes her contact details, tells her colleagues to ignore messages from him, explaining the situation to them in her sad, calm, endearing way, and everyone learns how to cope; life, inevitably, goes on. But her little brother's seizures don't stop and neither does the obsession burning away in his heart, and when he figures out that she's getting married to this guy in spite of everything that she's done to try to hide it from him, keeping it from all her social media accounts, which she barely uses anyway *because she's so fucking perfect*, and even warning friends not to say or post anything, something in his poor, confused mind cracks a little further and he leaves the city that he's grown up in and takes a long-haul bus all the way to Cambridge, Massachusetts, traveling across the wide American continent so as to be closer to her, and once there he takes his campaign of sexual harassment up to a whole new level and starts to do things like deface photographs of them together as children, scribbling over them with obscene drawings and suggestions and leaving them in her mailbox at the university, and relentlessly messages her friends and professors with his demented sexual fantasies, and, even worse, leaves great big sacks of feces outside the house where she lives with Brad. Finally, he begins to follow them down the street at a distance when they walk her fiancé's little white dog, until one day he somehow captures and strangles the dog and leaves it outside their front door, and when they find the tiny body they take it into their house and just break down and cry, and it's right at that moment that the older sister looks up at the window and sees that her younger brother is *peering in*—his crazed face is twisted with pleasure, and it takes no effort of the brain to deduce that he is jerking off, he's looking at them cradling the corpse of their little white dog and jerking off—and this perfect girl begins to feel as if her heart will break in two—that is to say, a great and terrible desolation overwhelms her—and she feels like she can't breathe, let alone speak, and so it comes as a total surprise to her when she hears herself say in a clear voice: 'If only—if only somebody would get Aquinas in here!'"

Mary finished her story with a flourish of her hands and Agathe laughed. "You're so good!" Mary smiled and walked to the window, her younger sister following at her heels. "You can see the whole camp!" Below them lay the beleaguered circle of the encampment, hemmed in on all sides by the forest. They could just about make out the contours of the tarmac road, something black glinting through the trees, but above all the world was an ocean of unfathomable green. The rotting wooden wall that surrounded the encampment was interrupted by the orange metal barriers of the former gate, a blue plastic sign trampled into the earth, now almost unreadable—FAKULTNÍ NEMOCNICE—and the low shape of the canteen humped to one side. Mary was about to say something to Agathe, to thrill in the fact of their transgression—that they were here, high above the Matriarch and without her knowledge—when her eye was caught by a dark shape dashing away from Jan's building. Another shape followed at a distance. The two of them watched Marta as she ran toward the wall of the encampment, Jan limping after her. She leaned against it, and by the time Jan reached her she was laughing. They began to speak, but neither Mary nor Agathe could catch the sense of what they said; all that floated up to the sixth floor of their mother's apartment block was an indistinct river of sound from which no individual words could be picked out. Soon Marta began to giggle again and Jan leaned forward, but she had already slipped away from him, leaping over the sagging wall before running into the forest, still laughing.

The Schoolmaster's Dilemma

The mound of fabric murmured to itself in the cool darkness of the schoolmaster's quarters, but instead of filling him with a calm sense of his progress through time, as the image of the mound so often did, the quiet, contented rustling of the moths as they burrowed into its warm core tugged at his thoughts, made him remember his distance from them, and grievances like bile rose in the corroded alley of his throat because the schoolmaster couldn't be sure if it was the sound and what it suggested that gave him no peace or something else entirely, a small voice that spoke above the thrum of his resentment and reminded him that everyone else was together and he was all alone; the children had not come for three days now but he felt no peace: everybody else was *celebrating*, and it was because of this that he had been forgotten; they were celebrating that witch and the origin story she toted around with her like a sack of old shit; they were eating and fucking and congratulating themselves on having escaped it, the disaster, the cataclysm, salvation, whatever she'd deemed it, and they were looking at their fat mother and the mess of the camp with gladness flooding their souls, happy to be alive in this hell, and he, the schoolmaster, was left alone with his wisdom and his moths and his unwavering belief that one day God would return and punish them for everything, but especially for this—for having the nerve to rejoice in their degradation, to celebrate their shame, and for leaving him all alone, a discarded toy, an abandoned, overweight doll. Now hatred washed over him. If only he still had his legs! He would skip through the forest, nimbly supporting his own wide girth, and tell them what he thought of them, before taking Dolores in his arms and carrying her back to his dark lair, and after the schoolmaster was done with her he would give her to the mound and the moths would rejoice, the mound would thrive, and he would wrap himself up in the crumbling blankets of the outermost layers and sleep the deep and contented sleep of the just. But he didn't have his legs, and there was no peace in his heart, only hatred for her and her children, and today the mound had shut him out, the moths talked only to themselves, the bread was stale—he was *alone*—and just as he was beginning to think that he couldn't endure another day like this, the schoolmaster became aware of a new impulse, and he understood that he wanted to go outside; and although he had not left his apartment by means of his own power for a long time, the schoolmaster also knew it wasn't impossible, and so quickly, not wanting the impulse to escape and leave him alone again, he crawled away from the mound and down the corridor that led to the outside world, using his strong upper arms to drag himself through the debris that lined the floor, leaves, dust, and dead flies; and sooner than he expected he found himself outside and the bright white mass of the sun pinned him down like an insect.

The schoolmaster looked into the black entrance hall of the apartment block behind him and remembered again that it had been years, a whole score of years, since he'd left the security of his nest unaccompanied by one of the children; it was the teaching of them, the building of the mound, and the endless wait for the coming of the God-moth—these things had exhausted him, and being so exhausted he had lost interest in the world beyond the apartment and the schoolroom; and though of course this was true and good because the mound was the repudiation of earthly life and the rejection of *worldliness*, now a sudden curiosity came over him, a yearning to see the city and the changes wrought upon it by time; he wanted to see the silent city and compare it to the city that he had known in his youth; the thought of decay aroused him; he wanted the sick satisfaction he would get from knowing that they couldn't cling on for much longer because following the return of Dolores it was obvious that their senile mother had had it at last and without her they would be doomed—it had to be over soon!—and besides, he was old; and so the schoolmaster crawled away from his home and through the streets of the dead city. It was warm, though the sun was not yet at its peak. By the sides of the road the abandoned cars were basking in the light, which gleamed across their dusty metal pelts, and the absolute quiet of the city was their purr: a soft, noiseless hum. It occurred to the schoolmaster that the city was alive in its own way and it was the case that these things—the cars with their shiny plastic eyes and the questioning, rectangular mouths of apartment blocks—were part of that life; the schoolmaster saw himself crawling down the wide street that they'd once called *Ječná*, a lonely fat figure moving between two lines of cars, and he felt their gaze upon him because the cars were watching and waiting and once the distance swallowed him up they would spring into motion again and whisper and squawk like gigantic roosting birds. Next the schoolmaster's eye was drawn to a trio of cars to his left, one an aging red, almost entirely brown with rust, and the other two dulling blue and green; each car had its own individual marking, a distinctive car-soul; yes, yes—the souls of objects!—and once the schoolmaster was lost from sight they would resume their thing-lives, racing along the empty roads with a silent roar, defueled, unvoiced, but held together by a secret power, the life that they'd kept hidden through all those years of ungrudging servitude; and the city—this unwound too—greeted them with a noiseless cry of its own—and the schoolmaster knew that to the cars the city was no necropolis but a living mutability full of living things, that on some plane invisible to the human eye the city was as fertile as a river delta; the death of humanity—this was their freedom— and he craned his head over his shoulder and looked at the cars behind him and something like jealousy tittered in the back of his mind.

If only he could change too! He would transform into a rusty black car, his human soul would dissolve, and the ineffable world of the objects would rise up around him; humbly, he would join his kind. For once in his life the old schoolmaster would be welcome. No, he had to remember: eventually, the mound would welcome him. Once the mound was satisfied, it would welcome him. He would escape the prison of his body, this legless ineptitude. Hope brought him back to himself and the taunt of the city was silenced. But another notion was beginning to form in the schoolmaster's mind and he thought it had something to do with water; it was the image of a delta that had done it. The schoolmaster began to crawl in the direction of the river, to where he imagined it curving away from him behind the screen of derelict buildings. He picked up his pace, suddenly eager, his thick arms propelling him forward and his enormous lungs forcing the air out of his body with the powerful hiss of a steam engine. His mind set ineluctably on the river, the schoolmaster negotiated his way through the narrow, twisting streets that lay between him and the water's edge.

When the river swam into his sight, shock hammered his body and deflated the schoolmaster like a balloon. His mouth and nose worked furiously to fill his chest with air and he squinted his watery eyes and tried to focus on the figure that he thought he saw in the distance. It leaned against a tree at the edge of the island in the middle of the river that interrupted the broad bridge halfway. What had that island been called? But the schoolmaster couldn't even remember the name of the city, and so he pushed the gibbering of his memory to one side and stared at the figure on the other side of the water. From this far away the schoolmaster couldn't tell if it was a man or a woman, but something about the way it leaned made him think of camels and hooded travelers passing through deserts of immeasurable size; of blue oases and the deep green fronds of palm trees; of coconuts, dates, and a slave boy with a jeweled fan—

no—what was he thinking—it was the light; it had caught him! But fear brought him into the present because the figure in the distance was so strange and out of place that it couldn't be right; and now the schoolmaster remembered that everybody else was dead, only he and Jakub ever entered the city, and the figure looking out across the river could not be Jakub because by now Jakub would have raised his hand or called the schoolmaster by name; and anyway, the dratted boy was celebrating with the rest of them, no doubt already in the arms of one of his sisters, and so the schoolmaster stopped and walled his mind up against the light and the slippage, and thought about what to do next.

Still—the figure was still—staring without stopping at the city before it, and the river was still too, a smooth and deadly surface—today there was no wind. And there was something in the absolute stillness of the mysterious figure that slicked the schoolmaster with nausea—motion being so integral to human life that surely the damned thing should have twitched by now or adjusted its weight by shifting from foot to foot. Inhuman—there was something inhuman about it, whatever it was that was watching him from the island in the middle of the river, a dark belt of water hemmed by a crust of empty buildings erupting into the still air, the dead efflorescence around them. Ah, death—perhaps the thing was dead, after all, and what the schoolmaster had interpreted as a living human figure was simply a great pink spool of flesh that did not *lean* against the tree but was *collapsed* upon it, and the abyss between those two words comforted the old schoolmaster because the quiet intentionality of *lean* had frightened him. Yes, yes, it was possible that the figure was dead and stared at the city with the calm eyes of the dead, and in that case the schoolmaster could approach the apparition without fear; it was a mirage, a river-ghost, some sad body belched up by the water; a drowned adventurer from a city he didn't know—German, perhaps—carried all the way into the enormous stone tomb of the city, *their* city, for him to find, another thing for his mound.

The schoolmaster hauled himself forward again with his eyes fixed on the opposite side of the water where the figure was collapsed (where the figure *leaned*) against the gnarled surface of the tree, the rough bark digging into skin made spongy by the interminable nature of the voyage that it had endured—and how the moths would love the soggy weight of it, the schoolmaster crooned to himself—yes, it wasn't *leaning*; nobody had said anything about *leaning*, and so he crawled along the stony length of the bridge and the whole time he kept his tiny eyes screwed up and his concentration sharp, angled toward the surprising reality of the figure on the opposite shore, which, he reiterated to no one in particular, still had not moved and so could not have been *leaning* and therefore was nothing, absolutely nothing to fear. As he drew closer the figure became more distinct, and the schoolmaster realized that what he was looking at was not a man at all, but a woman—there was something distinctly feminine about its bulk—yes, a woman, clothes still wet, plastered to her skin, who stared with lidded eyes out over the calm water, so still, herself in turn so still, probably dead, though this was conjecture because the schoolmaster couldn't see her face, he had to remember that he couldn't yet see her face; and he didn't think about why she might be dead in his city, but continued to crawl, grim and determined, his body exhausted by the atypical exercise and his elbows bloody; somewhere far away the mound was calling out for him.

But still the schoolmaster crawled onward. He reached the middle of the bridge and then found the narrow stone stairs that led to the overgrown park in which he'd spotted the figure. The sun sloped across the white sky and the light poured down, stronger now, more ardent. The schoolmaster pulled himself through the undergrowth toward the place where the figure rested, the big sodden body he'd seen from the other side of the water, his tongue darting out of his pink mouth and scraping along the cracked surface of his lips, and he wanted to laugh at how he'd felt earlier, so timid and full of fear. He skirted the edge of an old café and spotted the back of her head, blond hair, dark with water. It drooped forward, her chin resting on her chest—though he couldn't see it, he had to remember that he couldn't *see* her face, couldn't let the light slide through him like that—and she was so soft, so womanish, her long blond hair glued to her skull, a paste of hair, big shoulders sloping down; and then fear clammed up his heart again as he realized that she wasn't collapsed after all—rather, she was *pinned* to the tree, and that was even more sinister than *leaned*, was possessed of a whole different kind of intentionality—she was pinned to the tree by means of a metal pole that had been driven through her body on one side and went all the way through, smashing into the wood of the tree. A tremor passed over the schoolmaster because although he hadn't seen any other people around as he'd crawled through the city—only the sleeping, secretive cars—he suddenly became conscious of both the distance that separated him from his lair and the impossibility of escaping in his legless state if someone or something hostile were to happen upon him, and for a moment he couldn't understand why he hadn't thought of this before, but then he knew: it was the light—the light had deceived him, led him on; the schoolmaster's sudden impulse to leave the security of his quarters had belonged to nothing but the same disorder that had enveloped the encampment ever since the sending-away of Dolores, and the silent scream of the mound battered his ears.

Yes—the light had deceived him. The female shape of the damp body had lured him here: he'd imagined snuffling his face right up into those sodden folds before giving her to the moths and the mound and waiting for the sweet, musty smell of earthly decay to fill his quarters in the months to come. And in the depths of his fear the schoolmaster saw that he had strayed from the path delineated by the mound, that he'd succumbed to the temptations of the material world and the empty promises of the flesh, and, worst of all, he had wanted to cheat his way to salvation, had hoped that the gift of the body would win the mound over, spell the moths to speech; but this could never work because these were exactly the kind of tricks the mound had warned him *against*; and it hadn't been the river, after all, that had brought her here—no, this was no innocent corpse—but something else entirely, another *human*, though the idea that there could be anything beyond them and their world was inconceivable to the schoolmaster because of course that bitch had been lying about another group and her reasons for sending Dolores away had had nothing to do with anything except power, but now his thoughts were running away with him and whatever the schoolmaster thought about the Matriarch and her vision, it was a fact that the body lay before him and her meaning was a warning indexed to her like the number tag on an abandoned coat, the implications of which assailed the schoolmaster as he cowered behind the fan of his hands, not wanting to look at the big metal pole that slashed through her without mercy, and fear like acid bubbled at the back of his throat.

The sun beat down on his exposed nape.

Then the schoolmaster knew that he had never been meant to find her. Who could have guessed that he would choose to leave his nest on this day of all days, when everybody else was feasting and celebrating? It had been years since he had left his apartment by any means other than that of the metal wheelbarrow, and the only one of the children who dared to wander through the center of the city was Jakub. Perhaps Jakub had been meant to find her. Perhaps she had been left here as a sign for the others. This thought comforted him, as did the discernible age of the body—by now he could *smell* her—and from this distance the schoolmaster could see that her hair was flattened against the convexity of her skull by means of *blood*, not water. The schoolmaster crawled toward the pinioned female body, noting the way that her skin blackened around the intrusion of the metal pole. The shadow of the tree had lied to him— the body was a day or two old at least, and so perhaps nobody was watching him after all, and besides, who would want to harm a silly old schoolmaster? He squirmed in the sweaty cage of his black robes before gathering up the courage to circle the corpse. Her face was tumbled onto her chest, precisely like he'd imagined it, and as the schoolmaster craned to look at the lolling head with its straggling of blond hair he suddenly understood that he was looking at the mutilated body of *Marta*—her big, bold head toppled against the shelf of her bosom—Marta dead, singled out, separated from her siblings and the encampment and the cruelty that lay beneath it all, and looking into her bruised face the schoolmaster thought to himself that the history of the world was the history of cruelty, that it had never been anything else: they limped along the great curve of extinction, one foot in the void, dwindling each year, and it was *cruelty* that made them cling on, pain and the paining of others that kept them moving—yes, there had to be other settlements too, scattered along the empty swaths of land, the depopulated surface of the globe, because they could never give it up, life, cruelty, and so on and so on—and the schoolmaster thought he understood, briefly, *everything*.

Marta looked down at him; the city surged up around them. The schoolmaster was reassured by the familiarity of her features; the kinship between them was a wall thrown up against the encroachments of the city, the invasion of the light, and it didn't matter that she was dead—they were together. He reached out with one hand and touched her cold fingers with his own before hoisting himself upright against the tree and the body with its dead smell and beginning to *pull*—using the weight of his legless body as leverage, the schoolmaster tugged at the metal pole that pinned Marta to the tree.

The Schoolmaster's Body

That night Franta lay next to Mary with his weasely face all burrowed up in sleep, and though he started out dreaming about his older sisters and the ponderous way that they moved, like immense wooden sloops creaking across the surface of the ocean, now his thoughts coalesced around a little brown saint wandering through the forest with a white sheep at his side. All of a sudden he knew, his heart flashing with it, that the saint was Aquinas, and Franta wriggled with delight. He knew the little sheep from the covers of the videocassettes that they loaded into the player at the hour put aside for the show, the same day every week, because the Matriarch had never stopped insisting that some kind of order be imposed on the blank river of their time, and so she borrowed from the simple rhythms of her own childhood and pretended for the sake of that order that a broadcast cut through the crushing emptiness of forest, city, and sky at regular intervals. But what was Aquinas doing out here? Franta's eyes, like two old cameras, outflanked the saint and circled around. Hovering in front of him, he could see the

faint aureole that hung about Aquinas, and it struck him
then that this was not something that happened all at once
but was rather something *accrued* over time, like the layers of
sediment that eventually turn into rock, successive genera-
tions of painters slopping it around his beaming face until
one day, suddenly, it's there: a silty halo that he can't get rid
of, a saint's stink. Franta narrowed his eyes and tried to concentrate on the corporeal Aquinas. A wiry black beard pro-
truded from his fat chin, topped by the great, sweaty expanse
of his face, his broad temples, and curly dark hair. His small
eyes squinted in the fierce sunlight and the soft swell of
his belly blazoned spiritual ineptitude, his weakness for the
pleasures of the flesh and the lure of the material world.
How different he was from Franta's image of him! He had
imagined something more heroic.

As Aquinas waded through the sea of green ferns, Franta
heard the roaring of applause, the strange, inhuman howl
that is the emergent property of crowds. It came crashing
through the silent forest, so loud that he wondered how he'd
missed it before, and the scaffolding of a gigantic bleacher
appeared through the curtain of trees. Franta already recognized the scenario from a childhood spent sprawled out in
front of the Matriarch's blinking television, although he had
never approached it from this angle, with a perspective so
disembodied and free, and so he hurried past Aquinas because he wanted to see the shouting audience and the game
that tracked itself out across the bright green length of the
pitch. He slithered along the alley between the bleachers
sprouting out of the earth like huge wooden mushrooms—
yes, there was no sense in which they didn't belong here,

something whispered inside him, there was nothing here that didn't belong to the forest and the dead world he'd grown up in—and when he emerged from the shadows the players were beetling across the pitch in their bright livery while the audience above them squirmed in their seats, thousands and thousands of people, more than he'd ever seen before in his life. The ball hit the turf with a lurid orange swoop before ricocheting upward again. Behind him, Aquinas keeled in the shadows. The sheep snorted and shook its woolly head, and when Franta looked back at the two of them he thought that God had sent Aquinas the little white sheep as punishment for what he wrote about animals, though he couldn't explain how he knew this or even what it was that Aquinas had written, just that the information was accessible to him in the same way as other objects of general knowledge, such as his mother's red wheelchair, or the schoolmaster's lust for Dolores. But then he realized that he could see what Aquinas was thinking because his thoughts curled around his head in big bold letters that linked together to form sentences, loops of sentences, as if he were scrolling them out, everything around him in the process of being recorded, and despite the fact that Franta was not able to read, the sense of them was immediate and apparent because they were written in the very same garbled vulgate that he spoke with his siblings, the language that belonged to the light.

It was the soul that interested the sheep, Aquinas thought, looking down at its fluffy tail, which twitched and trembled with silent disapproval. The sound that came from the bleachers blocked out any other noise, and the crashing of applause was like the crashing of the ocean, waving through his mind. He breathed heavily and clutched his side. The obvious spirituality of the sheep, its superiority in such matters—it made sense that the challenges of the flesh left the smug little bastard unmoved. Yes, it was the prayers delivered daily in its secret sheepish tongue and the quiet winking down of gods so old that even Aquinas could not know them that saved the sheep, made it beam all over with soft, holy satisfaction, undaunted by either the quick march through the forest or the merciless white light that bored through the canopy, whereas Aquinas, red-faced and sweaty, leaned in the shadows beside one of the bleachers and pleaded with his God for a breather. Stupid animal! There was a reason why in the old days they'd been right at the bottom of the heap, imprisoned in the factory farms, the barren fields of the past, millions and billions of animals, tails docked, ears clipped, children stolen, stunned, shredded, plucked to nothingness—yes, a reason, and now his mind groped for it, and it had something to do with their *lack* of reason, their small brains and mute tongues, although they vocalized, that much was true, but whatever logic they had was alien because just look at the way the sheep went about things, just look at how it put its freedom to work. It looked up at Aquinas, its head tilted to one side. This mute world was their revenge, perhaps what He'd meant all along, when He'd promised (so long ago now! a pain in his chest) the meek their inheritance. But the sheep had never been meek—only quiet, brooding, and waiting for its moment.

Franta looked away from Aquinas and began to watch the game, but soon enough the little referee ran to the center of the pitch and began to whistle without stopping. The players thudded to a halt, confused. The audience squealed in protest. High up on the bleacher nearest Franta the manager of the team who currently had the advantage scratched at his balding head. There was no sign of a foul, no sign that the invisible lines of the game had been transgressed in any way, and the ancient order was true, realer than ever, they all knew that much, but it started to seem to them as though he were hymning it, as if the squall of his whistle was a threnody to what they had left behind, reminding them of what lurked beyond the screen of the game, waiting for them in the quiet green forest that pressed too close. The image of the pitch began to waver and Franta was starting to see what lay behind it, the suggestion of a field, Jan's field, the same dull promise of growth as always, only now interrupted . . .

The referee's face reddened, became apoplectic. The ball was as still as a rock. "Make him stop!" yelled a beefy man up in the bleachers, twisting in his seat and pressing his thick thighs together. The audience repeated his cry uneasily—"Make him stop!"—but the referee continued to blow into his whistle, the sound of which was a long, drawnout wail from hell, and the players writhed in the short green grass, making snakes with their arms. The audience groaned. He kept on whistling, and the sound of the whistle became a rasping that made Franta think of a nest of wasps hanging in the rafters of a dusty forgotten barn. Behind him Aquinas was brooding again, wasps in his mind too. In this vanquished world the animals had won; the only real metaphors left belonged to them, because even dead they were living, and it was them who reeled the world back, fluvial, straight back to the middle years of the Paleocene, long before the appearance of the first humans, the first real humans who would, human-like, kill off all their nearest relatives. Back to the relative quiet of prehistory, the fantastic plants, untroubled megafauna, and the slow dream of life; the absolute silence of the denuded polar north in which the sun was lost, drowned, reduced to stray iceblink, the dim gleam of the horizon; vague, algal significance. Aquinas crouched behind the bleacher but it didn't look like he was planning on going anywhere anytime soon. The sheep looked away. The sun screeched down. The sound and the heat were unbearable. Franta thought that he was ready. He coughed and stepped out from the shade of the bleacher. Implausibly, they heard him, ten thousand eyes arrowing down on his head. "I know what we should do," Franta said. "We should GET AQUINAS IN HERE—"

And the world folded in on itself, just like that.

***

Jan stared at the dry earth and thought about rain. Although the sun was crouching over the forest and the field, in the encampment the others were still asleep. Hidden away in the dark dormitories, they dreamed through the crisis closing in on them, because, he thought, giving in to the rhythms of his interior monologue, if the rain didn't come, then the crops would fail, and if the crops failed, there would be almost nothing to eat through the cold winter, the land around the encampment having been plundered almost entirely; and it was also the case that if the rain didn't come and his crops failed, then the same devastation would strike the forest too; it would dry up, and the dim, crawling life that had held on against all odds in the poisoned earth would disappear, and neither he nor his family would be able to do anything to stop it. It would be a long, hungry winter, Jan concluded, and the image of a centipede crawled into his brain and buried its flat head in the soft gray matter. If only it would rain! If only the rain would come and fill the dry basin of the earth—the land west of the wall that he himself had so lovingly cultivated, on which he had pinned his hopes—and lay the foundations for those uniform lines of green shoots, which would tell him that despite everything—the poison, the invisible lime of the dead world—he was right to believe in them, in the capacity of the earth to renew itself. It would be a long and hungry winter, yet the ploy of agriculture had worked in the past, he knew that much, and he had fed his sprawling family through many other winters. He closed his eyes and saw them, his sisters with their pregnant bellies sweating in the summer heat, their broad shoulders supporting the weight of the plow or their coarse hands pollinating the adult plants because the few bees left were as lazy as his younger siblings, and he heard the thumping of their powerful steps as they lurched along the length of the field, working in pairs through spring and summer, pushing, always pushing, his big, brave girls, breaking up the hard surface of the soil so that life could squirm through. How he'd loved watching them, with their wide peasant faces and dimpled knees. But when he opened his eyes the field was empty. The rain had betrayed them. There had been no rain and there would be no rain and Jan didn't know what to do.

At night he dreamed of an infinite field and the dream filled him with agony, because how could he be expected to water it all with the supplies he had, nothing but dirty river water and a temperamental old well? And so the field would become a greater dying than ever before. All of a sudden he couldn't manage the thought of it any longer, and his mind fled back to the encampment baking in the fierce heat and the room in which his mother lay with her sunglasses pushed to one side, a soft, dewy sheen on her skin, and their uncle flat out on the floor next to her bed. Jan pictured him crawling to her side, a white handkerchief on his bald head, ready to nuzzle away at her like a disgusting old dog, saliva hanging in strands from his open mouth, and the way that the strands caught in the chapped, broken skin of his lips disgusted Jan: he thought that in some way even this was unmoist, as though the dense liquid their uncle exuded from his mouth at the sight of his sister did not belong to the ordinary secretions of men and their passions. But then his mind recoiled from its image—he had never dared before to imagine his mother lying down, nor their uncle approaching her, his ideas confined always to the lines that the Matriarch herself had laid out, a system of possible notions. Something was unwinding, coming loose in his head. Jan's eyes began to film. The Matriarch had kept them together in spite of everything, the children, the camp, the field, and the rain that had come in regular intervals, at all times holding it before her: an imaginary tower, her wooden citadel. They lived because she had willed it, and though the memory of her extreme generosity rarely failed to fill Jan's heart with joy, now he couldn't stop thinking about that story, the past she shared with his uncle and what they did in the dark, and he was tortured by jealousy and rage because Jan couldn't stand to see his mother brought low, had never wanted to know anything about the sinewy, unnatural love that had birthed them all. He saw his mother in his uncle's arms and moaned. If only the rain would come and clean everything away, wash away the dust and grime of the summer, the sweat of their mutual sins, and limn them with forgiveness. And then the green seedlings were in his mind again, and tears welled up in the cracks of his eyes. He rubbed at them with his sleeve. It was because of Dolores—it was her fault that the crops were failing. Stupid cow. And it was because of Marta too. Jan wasn't sorry that the little bitch was gone. But it was because of her that the Matriarch had walled herself up in her dark office, their uncle at her feet, thinking, thinking, and all the while doubt spread through the encampment like a disease. Soon the others would begin to question the routine for which he had given everything. They were questioning it already, and Jan revolved around a single point of agony because he hadn't liked their mother's new story one bit, or the desperate, confessional impulse he had seen in her eyes. Another dry and rainless day. Yes, they were being punished for something.

Agathe watched Jan from behind a pile of sticks. He knelt in the failed promise of the field without noticing her and thought in hard, dry images that nicked at her mind. He belonged to the dirt, she decided, was separated from it only by time and the dim quality they called reason, but the stalled motion of his figure disquieted her because she had always associated Jan with the implacable forward movement that belonged to their mother and the pitched battle of the encampment, and so this strange kneeling was part of the confusion that had swept over them all since Dolores's return. By now she was thinking in the long, looped sentences she associated with a fear she scarcely knew, and this was because for once in her life Agathe could barely stop thinking, clear, precise thoughts that astounded her, and each thought connected to another and there was no end to them. She covered her face with her hands so that she wouldn't have to look at anything, not Jan in the dirt nor the invisible rows of his imaginary crops, but still she was full of sentences, and around her the world was brighter than ever, glinting sharp and dangerous, everything unbearably distinct with nothing to flatten it; objects repelled her and she glanced off them, and although it was a relief for once not to be so caught up in things, Agathe knew that this, too, had something to do with the language that had invaded her head, which was the expression of her mother's way of seeing, crammed with edges. What she saw was shorthand, a summary; the excess was pared away. Out on the field Jan was a spike of flesh that was having nothing to do with anything else, and it was terrible to look at him. She rolled onto her back and stared at the sun, blinking away her tears and squinting until she was positive that she could see it, the true sun, a disk that was even brighter than the surrounding sky, and then she closed her eyes because she couldn't bear it any longer and waited for the pain in her head to subside. When she opened them again it was as if the field and the surrounding trees had been painted black, and Jan, still kneeling, was a dark granite monument, her own arm the color of gray mud. And somewhere she didn't know about Marta was rotting quietly, and her pink skin would take on the same hue, which was concord, the color of the universe, a sameness that could only be discerned by means of this passage between worlds, the portal of the sun, cold murder; the pain in her eyes was worth it, Agathe concluded, because now she saw the world as it was: a timeless plane on which they were pinned like insects, and something lay flat behind it, not quite wanting to show its face, and this was her uncle's god, who at all times hid behind a blinding play of surfaces. Stalled—they were all stalled—in the dead space between events, the encampment with its order trailing out behind it like a broken net.

She thought about the others.

In the stone dormitory, Mary was crying with her face pressed up against the mattress. She had dreamed of the men who would come for Dolores and who had taken Marta, because now that her sister was gone her skepticism was too, and she could see that their mother's error was bigger than they could have ever imagined. There were no lessons, and no work either; the days were beginning to lose their shape.

On the other side of the square, Alexandra and Eva were tearing out pages from one of the schoolmaster's books and talking about Marta, whom they hadn't seen since the night their mother had tried to win them over with her story.

Slumped in her chair, the Matriarch was thinking that the farther away objects were from her the more indistinct they became. She rubbed at her tired eyes and the black lenses of her sunglasses stared up at the ceiling.

Shut in their tower, Jan's sisters were idling. In the long

week that followed their mother's telling of her story, Jan had shown no desire to drag them out to the field, and it was pointless anyway because the sudden brutality of the sun had no precedent in their lives: the rains had not come, though they had always been reliable as clockwork, and the field was a desert, as dead as it got. Their brother was nowhere to be seen and their children ran wild.

Inside the sunny schoolroom, Franta was stalking one of Jan's beloved chickens, scuttling across the floor like a crab on his thin knobbly legs, his stiff arms extended out to his sides as if to catch some phantom breeze. He imagined what it would be like to eat one: pink flesh blackening, skin crackling, thrust into the fire—and the smell!—and saliva pooled in his mouth. But he was afraid of their older brother, who guarded his chickens jealously; the siblings felt his bleary pig eyes upon them wherever they went: they saw them in the peeling wood that lined the windows of their mother's apartment block, or in the brown fronds of parched ferns, watching them as they scurried through the forest on one of the trips to forage supplies from the abandoned shopping centers, or as they worked in the field, his eyes studded into the hard, reproachful earth. And so as soon as he got close, Franta would dart away again, and the chicken clucked calmly as though the world were empty of threat, which, of course, it wasn't.

And last of all Jakub, Adam, and Marek were walking along the crumbling path to the city with the metal wheelbarrow creaking in front of them. By the time it had finally occurred to the three boys to fetch the old schoolmaster, over a week had passed since the Matriarch's disastrous ceremony, and so they sloped along guiltily.

Down in his dark basement room the schoolmaster was perched on a table with his chin resting on the ledge of the high rectangular window. This was his only point of contact with the outside world now that he had barricaded both the inner door of his sanctum and the outer door of the apartment block. His sentinel eyes were level with the earth, and when the boys emerged from the trees the schoolmaster was ready for them. He listened as they examined the wall of furniture blocking the corridor, which as far as he was concerned was insurmountable, and when the three of them circled back to observe the building at a distance and caught sight of the schoolmaster's gloating face inside its frame of window, he enjoyed, too, the surprise that widened their idiot eyes. Jakub moved toward the apartment block, but before he could say anything the schoolmaster cut him off with a little squeal. Then he said commandingly, "I'm not coming with you!" Inside his window the schoolmaster was numinous. Jakub stepped back, dumbfounded. Marek interjected, "It's time for the lesson—" but the schoolmaster was already castling away from them. "There won't be any more lessons," he said, and the three boys exchanged glances. Marek tried again, "But our mother—" while Adam looked around as if he thought he could find the source of the schoolmaster's power, only the city was the same as always, silent, inward-eyed. A foul smell had begun to float up from the basement. The schoolmaster risked a glance back to the mound behind him, and when he looked at the boys again his eyes were bright, arrowed by love. Jakub walked over to the window and examined the schoolmaster's pale, hectic face. He said, cautiously, "You'll run out of supplies."

The schoolmaster giggled. He had everything he needed—the mound and Marta. As he had waited for the boys to come, it had struck him that even if he were to tell them they would barely be able to understand the fact of her death, because although the schoolmaster would like to deny it a strange and inscrutable power had hung over the encampment all of these years, as if the Matriarch had been taking direction, and he didn't know what to call it, the cushioning of her faith, but difficulty had never crushed them in the way the schoolmaster thought they deserved, as if the family were something fated and each sibling a fixed star in the firmament; when they were born it was as though they had always been there, everything in order, no real growth beyond the first possibility and no real diminishment either, despite what their mother said. If she'd wanted change, she'd had to manufacture it. Had anybody really died before? Could anybody really die anymore? The schoolmaster couldn't remember. He hadn't understood how he had gotten through the years, and nor had he understood the force that their mother insisted was behind it all, the inward goad. Outside, the children watched him without impatience, only a slight bemusement and the slow, predatory waiting that belonged to their kind, as though they were expecting orders from that same authority whose presence the schoolmaster had often intuited but whose nature remained a mystery to him, only for once he wasn't afraid of it—the imaginary tower!—because every thing had been silenced at last; all around him the world was humbled and hardly daring to move.

Of course, before long the gossipy old schoolmaster couldn't resist telling them. "I found her by the river," he began, and the boys crowded close to listen.

Back in the encampment the light was slithering in through the broken plastic blinds of their mother's office, though they struggled against it, down to where their uncle lay on the floor beneath the window. There was no sound from the encampment expiring in the heat outside, and he thought it was because the children were waiting too, listening to the rumors about Marta's fate that were percolating through the semisolid air. He looked across the room at his sister and imagined escaping at last. But their uncle was so heavy that it seemed impossible to him that he had ever been capable of lifting himself up; now when he tried to raise his body from the floor he trembled with exertion, his arms wrestling with the mass of his torso, and his long, thin neck with the knotted stigma of his head. Their uncle returned his face to the floor and listened to the sound of his sister's boots hitting the stone as she paced along the length of the room. He knew he had always been weak, incapable of standing up to her, and that this was why he was so tired; it was punishment for his hubris, the ease of his former motion, because in the end he had squandered it. What had he accomplished? Nothing more than the prolonging of a general misery. Their uncle imagined a boy, a young boy with blond hair who sat next to him on the concrete floor and looked up at the Matriarch with curious eyes. The child would turn toward him and whisper into his ear—*Isn't she supposed to be in a wheelchair?*—and he would reply in a low whisper of his own that, no, his sister didn't need it, nothing had ever slowed her down: the wheelchair was a front, a calculated expression of vulnerability, a sign of what she had sacrificed for them, the endless and agonizing inconvenience of birth; and away from the eyes of her children she paced and paced, and she paced because she was frightened, the imaginary blond boy could intuit that much at least, contra to the naïveté of his big blue eyes, which, their uncle realized, were the eyes of his dead wife, and he felt the same pain as always, because the blond boy was a lie, a trick of the light, a way for memory to get at him. Now he saw her face because the boy had peeled away his own; the sound of his sister's footsteps receded into the distance and he stared into the face of his dead wife, their aunt—ah, but it wasn't her, it was never her, she'd been dead for years. Her image was already running away from him—it was only the calm blue eyes that remained in his memory like an open wound and the rest of her was blurred and falsified, her skin the dead matte of computer-generated imagery, because he'd made her up, he couldn't remember her properly, and it was the light that had done it: the world was a great lisp through which other lies and half-truths could slip, their reality only proximate, dwindling.

Their uncle lifted his hand to the exposed side of his face and let out a wail. The Matriarch stopped and turned her gaze on him. "What's the matter?" She walked over to where he lay on the floor and knelt beside him, brushing her stubby fingers against his cheek. His skin was cool to the touch. She raised her hand to her own burning face. Soon the schoolmaster would be here, she told herself, and the thought of his round, portly body hung in her mind like a bead. When he arrived she would get the answers she needed. After all, he had found Marta's body, or so he had said—"dead by the river, a metal pole going through her"— but when her sons had pressed onward into the city looking to corroborate his claim, they had found nothing but a shadow of dry blood. But what the three boys had told the Matriarch in their insolent way had frightened her because she couldn't help it, that maternal quavering, and she could guess at the reasons behind the schoolmaster's uncharacteristic behavior—safe in his window with a wall of furniture, and the *stench*—even if she scarcely dared to. Although her sons had refused to lay hands on the old schoolmaster, and the Matriarch had not been able to locate Jan, this had proved no hurdle to her will because her eldest daughters were still loyal. They remembered the way to the city from their own long childhoods, before Jan and the endless tedium of their tower, and now they were hurrying him to her; she imagined the schoolmaster tucked up beneath a traveling blanket of heavy, moth-eaten wool, his dark robes plastered to his clammy skin with sweat, and her daughters laughing as they went.

The Matriarch stroked the dome of her brother's skull and wrapped his wispy hair around her fingers. She was dimly aware of a development and knew that the others were too. In the square outside her window Dolores was playing in the dust, quivering with anticipation. Yes, her children were aware of something, tuned, as they were, like animals to incipient change.

When they knocked on the door the Matriarch walked back to her electric wheelchair and climbed into the high seat. She waited for them to knock again before answering. "Come in." Marketa stuck her face past the door. Her eyes scanned the room, took note of their uncle lying on the floor, and then darted upward to the pale, queenly figure of their mother. She pushed the door open, enough so that the Matriarch could see the crowd of her daughters and the metal wheelbarrow standing in the dirt beside the stone steps that led to her office, and then there was a soft thump as they tumbled the legless body of the schoolmaster onto the concrete floor of the threshold and kicked him inside. As he sputtered and groaned, her daughters withdrew, a flash of a smile from Marketa, then the quick closing of the door. For a moment there was no sound except for the quiet moaning of the schoolmaster on the floor and the thudding of her own heart as she sat in her throne and waited for someone to speak. But who could it be but her to break the silence, the Matriarch reminded herself, because she was the one who was in charge around here, shepherd to them all, and so it would be the Matriarch who would shepherd events to their conclusion, and this idea surprised her because she'd never thought willingly of a conclusion before, this being the very thing that had filled her with fear; now she reflected that a conclusion was something different from an ending—but her mind was running away from her again, unspooling—it was the light, the flood she dreaded, and so she leaned across the wooden desk and slatted the blinds as best she could. When she looked back at the schoolmaster his eyes were peeking at her from above the black disorder of his beard, and he was fat, enormously fat, fatter than ever, and the Matriarch realized that she could not explain how the schoolmaster had managed to thrive throughout those years alone in the city and away from her project, as if he didn't need them at all. The schoolmaster had stayed fat, even put on weight, and this, combined with the clipping of his legs and the lopsided heft of his body, made her think of an overstuffed teddy bear.

The Matriarch brightened up. "What happened to Marta?" she asked. The clock on the wall ticked away unevenly. The schoolmaster took his time in answering her. The girls had mistreated him: they had torn down his wall and dragged the schoolmaster from his den, and he had been bounced back to the encampment with no dignity at all, and now he was whiny and exposed. "I already told the others. There's nothing else to say, and I'm tired—" "I want you to tell me what you told them," the Matriarch insisted, and the schoolmaster whined again. "It will be the same, exactly the same." She repeated her question, "What happened to Marta?" The schoolmaster began to defend himself. "I was asleep, asleep in my room. I don't know anything. I found her like that, by the side of the river with a big pole going through her body." He paused and tried again. "She was on the island." The Matriarch looked at him and said nothing. Down on the floor their uncle extended one long arm and reached for a rag of light. But there was nothing that could be touched; his fingers clutched at the empty air and the sun robbed his hand of detail. Nothing from outside either—nothing save that slow and deadly waiting. The Matriarch prayed for a sound, a sign, the sharp snapping of branches as Marta made her way back to the encampment, not dead after all, and then everything could go back to how it was before because the Matriarch hadn't appreciated how lucky they had been, she had forgotten to be grateful. But her daughter was dead, the schoolmaster had said so, and he had no reason to lie, nor the inventiveness to do so. As they sat there the silence wore away at them both: the schoolmaster shifted his bulk from one hip to the other and the movement tugged the soft protrusion of his belly across the concrete floor, and something about this imperfect rotation made the Matriarch think about stars slipping their orbits, disorder—and when the schoolmaster spoke again she was surprised because she had grown used to it—this strange, restless silence. "I found her by the edge of the water. Of course, I didn't know that it was her at first. Nobody is ever in the city." The Matriarch interrupted him, sharp again. "But why were you in the city? You never leave your quarters. You don't have legs." The schoolmaster was sullen. "I can move—I can *creep*." The Matriarch continued. "It must have been difficult for you to crawl that far, all the way to the river. And the island is near the old theater, so you must have crawled along the shore too. I know you wouldn't go that close to the center. What made you decide to go to the river? How did you know where to find her?" The schoolmaster looked up at the Matriarch, and smiled a quick, secretive smile that she didn't like at all. "I was obeying orders," he said, and their uncle laughed. The schoolmaster repeated himself. "She was dead, very dead—a great metal pole all the way through her." The Matriarch asked, "She was dead when you found her?" He was indignant. "I didn't hurt her!" The Matriarch sighed. "I don't think you hurt her. I can't imagine you managing to hurt her. But the boys were confused. She was dead, you found her, the big metal pole. I'm not arguing with this. I wanted to know why you had to be the one to find her, but I should have known that you wouldn't be able to tell me. Even if you'd seen something or heard something, how would you be able to remember it in your state? Nothing but the same old nonsense as always. I shouldn't have expected anything from you; I'm seeing things more clearly now. But there's something else, something important. Where did the body go? It isn't where you said it would be." The body. The schoolmaster's black button eyes narrowed and the stumps of his legs tensed underneath the sheath of his robes. He had known that she'd ask about the body, had known that the question would come, and he could answer it, too, because he knew the body intimately, remembered the big, soppy weight of it in his arms as he'd lovingly dragged it back up the incline of the street, guided, perhaps, by the same mysterious power that had once guided the Matriarch, as if the mound were behind him, urging him on, his face pressed up against the dank skin of her neck—yes, she had been *heavy*, not with water, but with death. The silence of the city, the wailing of the mound, the buried facts of her murder—these things had not troubled him, his fear replaced by greed, sudden greed, and so he'd crawled and crawled without tiring, bloody palms against the burning tarmac of the road and her white, wormy body trailing behind him like the deflated sail of a ship. When he'd gotten her home, the moths had been waiting, and the mound was thick with anticipation. Where did the body go? Ah, but how could the schoolmaster answer her? How could he explain his actions to her cold, dispassionate mother, who, however cold, however dispassionate, could not fail to be outraged by his subsequent desecration—yes, that was what she would call it—of her daughter's body. The schoolmaster had given Marta to the mound, had pushed her deep into its dusty folds toward the heat at its center, and he'd dreamed of climbing in there too, of wrapping his arms around Marta's corpse and her hair, stiff with blood, cracking across his flushed cheek. He had dreamed of joining her, and the tears had coursed down his cheeks as he'd watched her disappear into the heart of the mound, her soft, buttery skin, yellow in the electric light, sliding away from his sight—alone again—and after the deed was done he gave himself over to an intermittent and feverish sleep taunted by dreams, memories of intimacy. Yes, he knew the body intimately, and the bitch had dragged him here to find out where it had gone; he wouldn't tell her. The light in the room was swallowed up by her sunglasses. If only he'd had the sense to stay at home! But what choice did he have, with that pack of harpies at his door? The schoolmaster didn't say anything. Their uncle lifted his head off the floor, exchanged a glance with his sister, and then said, in a perfect mimicry of the schoolmaster's own insolent falsetto, "He doesn't like it when we talk about bodies!" The heat, claustral, pressed in. The Matriarch steepled her hands. "What did you do to Marta's body?" One day all of them would die. One day history would catch up with them. This thought comforted the schoolmaster as he looked at the floor. If only some flood—and now he quivered with excitement—would come crashing over the green trees and gray buildings and sweep them all away; if only the deity would return and clean up His mess. He saw the golden flicker of a moth, the paler gold of Marta's hair. The arrow of the bitch's hands, leveled toward him—what had he done with the body? He'd given Marta to the mound, gifted her body to the God-moth, and now she was being transformed into something alien and new. Jealousy gnawed at his heart. It went like this: she would shuck off the thick swaddling of her skin, and the segmented white body of a larva would emerge and still be Marta, in the first stages of her salvation, and he would nurse this giant larva, feed it tiny scraps of silk, and she would be humble, like she never was in life, the old life—she would be *humbled*—and he would hold the white larva in his arms and whisper his secrets to the hard red gem of her head, and although she wouldn't say anything back he would be comforted by the slick weight of her and want for nothing. Blind and deaf—she would be saved, in his arms.

"What did you do to the body?" The schoolmaster looked back at the Matriarch. She leaned forward in her red chair. The schoolmaster made his decision. He said, "I took the body." The Matriarch frowned. "Where?" she asked him, and their uncle peered at the schoolmaster through his dirty lenses. On the other side of the door Jakub, his ear against the metal, pricked up. The schoolmaster was busy dumbfounding them, filled with shameless pride. "I took the body back to my quarters. I was lonely." He thought he could hear her mind spinning like a top. Their uncle asked, "Is the body still in your quarters?" Suddenly the light beamed through the slatted prayer of the window, and he knew that they'd never take her away from him, it was already too late, and in the hallowed darkness of his quarters the white larva was waiting, and this thought ate the heart out of his fear, beatified him: the fat moon of his face lit up with a holy inner light, and the Matriarch and her brother recoiled with an equally sudden disgust. There's no talking to these people, the schoolmaster thought to himself, and Jakub trembled with laughter on the other side of the door. Marta, the mound—nothing ever made sense around here! Their uncle turned away. The Matriarch looked out the window. Then Jakub fell backward with a yowl. When he opened his eyes the first thing he saw was Jan, crouched above him with his mighty hands clenched into fists. A sudden quiet, flat with menace, swept through the dark corridors of the apartment block.

Jan punched him and the pain was blinding. Jakub thought he heard the high wail of the schoolmaster but couldn't be certain—everything was dissolved into pain and light. His older brother began to drag him down the corridor to the stone platform in front of the apartment block, where Jakub knew he would beat him in full sight of everybody and make an example of him for daring to listen in, though by now this was the least of their transgressions. For a moment Jakub thought that once he got his breath back he could try to reason with their brother or even say that the whole thing was one big misunderstanding, and so he made himself limp as Jan pulled him down the corridor by his ankles. While Jan fumbled with the door, Jakub took the chance to look up at his brother. Beneath the dark brown disk of his face Jan was pale and his burly arms were thinner, the big muscles slack, drooping toward the earth in soft, fleshy wings. He was mumbling something that Jakub couldn't hear: each individual word was lost in the great shuffling and shifting of his speech, and it was as if he were chewing up their language and spitting it out again in even looser particles of meaning. He was mad, Jakub realized, beyond words and reasoning; all he wanted to do was hurt someone until they died. In an instant they were outside and the sun was above them. Jakub tried to scream, but no sound came out, nothing but pain and light, and Jan began to kick him as if he were hoping to break every single one of his ribs.

The Matriarch sat in her office and listened to Jakub suffer. The thudding of Jan's boots as they made contact with his body matched the rhythms of her own anxious heart. Nothing—nothing would remain of them, she decided, because now she could smell the coming change, which was the ripe, wet smell of her daughter's body, and there would be no escaping it. Marta was dead, and so she was content to let Jakub scream, to let Jan kill him and mash his insolent little face into a bloody pulp, because if she were to let him die then perhaps this would appease the invisible enemy, dissuade it from action, although Jan's brutality, too, was another kind of anomaly. It was not implausible that the death of one sibling could atone for the deviance of another—but if that was the case, then what of Marta?—and the Matriarch thrilled, saw the smooth ranks of enemy forces break line. No, it would never be like that. She was desperate. She

wanted to discover a pattern that would save her, and thinking like this was dangerous and superstitious, because if the
years after the disaster had shown her anything it was that
nothing was connected, nothing could be made to cohere
except through the objective trickery of her own actions, the
real-world imposition of her belief or will, which was by no
means *necessary*, and so she couldn't allow herself to weaken,
to start perceiving meaning where there was none, to surrender the grueling, imaginative labor of keeping them afloat,
the family going—life's venture! She couldn't allow herself
to forget that they were alone, nothing else out there, nothing but the mask of her paranoia and the slow drip of her
isolation, and the threat that faced them was not the threat
she had dreamed up at all but something else altogether,
something more entrenched and far more fatal, because Jan,
angered by the failure of her promises to them, had waylaid
Marta in the forest and impaled her by the side of the river,
and that was all there was to it.

The Excluded
Sublime (i)

Paint peeled away from wood, animated by light and heat. A beetle crawled through the dust and was observed: a big gray eye pushed itself closer and licked up the image. The corrugated gleam of the beetle's back was lost, for a single moment, within the black immensity at the eye's center, before reemerging again, scurrying brightly across the stretch of earth that sloped away from the dark wall. The eye watched the beetle until it disappeared from sight, and then it directed its gaze to the place where the shape of the building pummeled into the brown dirt and saw that the border was not so pure after all, the line of the concrete seamed with fine cracks and dotted with yellow patches of lichen, and when the eye moved closer still the line broke down into even smaller fragments: specks of gray matter and a white mold that furred the proximate ground. It was not clear where the wall ended and the earth began, and Dolores placed her heavy head on the surface of the world and closed her eyes. When she opened them again everything was different: the soft gray concrete was the ground and a grainy brown wall of earth leapt up into the blue sky. Everything belonged to everything else—nothing was distinct.

Dolores yawned and pressed her fist into her mouth. She wriggled in the warm dirt like a grub and the light pressed in on her, painting her pale skin pink with burn. She didn't want to be indoors, in the close heat of the room that she shared with her siblings. There was something inside her that kept her awake and filled her with a restless, nervous energy that was not her own. Out here it was better: she was absorbed by the slow drama of sky, wall, earth, and beetle, and the sun was almost wiping her out entirely. Dolores closed her eyes and began to droop. She felt as though she were loitering in some vast entrance hall, or hovering at the threshold of a long, sunlit corridor. Somewhere behind her Jakub was screaming, and the sounds that emerged from his bloody mouth were glassy orbs that rose through the air, light as bubbles, and although she could hear Jan and the mumbled prayer of his curses, Dolores was unafraid, caught, as she was, in this space between worlds. But she knew what Jan looked like, and in the beetle's absence his face came into her mind with a slopping, seasick lurch. Something else— the words and sounds that she couldn't form with her own disobedient mouth delivered to her now in her mother's clipped voice, "It was an *invasion*—": Jan's head tilted forward and the brown leather peak of his hat slipped down; a visor of shadow fell across his eyes, knighting him. His blows rained down on Jakub with righteous anger—the image of his younger brother pressed up against the wooden door, his face slack with the mean, smirking idiocy that belonged to the younger children, who didn't respect the Matriarch or his system, fed the fury in his heart. A red bubble of blood rolled over Jakub's lower lip. His brother had fainted. Jan wasn't sure how long he'd been beating him; he'd lost all track of time. The encampment was silent, save for Dolores, who was playing in the dust near the edge of the apartment block. Jan looked back at Jakub, who was curled up on the ground with his head lolling out to one side. Dolores—old poor-in-the-world Dolores—began to sing in a high wheedling voice that reminded him of Marta.

The beetle was back; she wanted to talk to it, but she didn't know how. Dolores smiled and the beetle crawled closer, craning its black antennae toward her. She opened her mouth and burbled something wordless and indistinct, the beginnings of a beetle-song, the matter of her mind working itself into the shape that she saw before her: the sounds that she made were hard, black, and shiny, and her gray eye darkened with a borrowed purple, the glossy aubergine gleam of the beetle's shell. She laughed, shivered with delight.

Jan toppled to the ground beside Jakub and the dust exploded around him. Dolores turned her head to look. Adam stood above Jan and in his hands he held a rusty metal pole, red with blood. He leaned forward to inspect their older brother, cautious but unafraid. Soon their siblings came streaming into the sunny square, Alexandra, Eva, Mary, and Marek hurrying toward them with Franta and Agathe trailing behind, and then even some of Jan's own sisters trickled into view. They formed a circle around the three brothers and their faces were calm with the expectation of murder. Adam shrugged and stepped forward and drove the pole down into the back of Jan's leg: the bone broke and the joint shattered. Their brother howled with his face in the dirt, and his leg flopped like a dead brown fish. The sound of his screaming woke Jakub, who squinted up at Adam from beneath the caul of one inflated eyelid and hauled himself into a sitting position. He saw the defeated shape of his older brother and took in the mashed knee, the bloody worm of his ruined leg, and smiled.

The siblings moved closer—the circle tightened. The whole lot of them must have been there, the great knot of the family, and maybe it was the case that they'd spent the last few decades waiting for a scene like this, for Jan to get his comeuppance, and it was with this in mind that they had endured the mummery of the encampment: the lessons, the farming, the fetching of water and the emptying of latrines, the squealing monotony of birth; the whole damned performance of survival. They'd waited and waited and the whole time this had been in their minds—the splattered melon leg with its exposed white ligaments glinting in the sunlight. And now they gathered and watched with the taut joy of fulfilled promises, met demands.

Adam struck Jan again, and the sharp crack of his hip as it broke hung in the air like an afterimage. He made a sound that was the bud of a scream, and his siblings looked on with shining eyes. The beatings and the leg—the asymmetry of vengeance. Jan, denuded, lay before them. A voice broke the silence. "He won't last long with a leg like that," said Franta, and they rubbed their eyes with their fists. The circle loosened and something like shame sprang up in the gaps between them, given strength by the silence—the too-decorous silence—from their mother's quarters. The light and the heat; their faces wrinkled, recoiled from one another. One by one they slunk away like dogs.

* * *

Eventually Dolores remembered that she had wanted to look. She crawled across the square in the direction of the stone platform before the apartment block where Jan lay dying. How much time had passed since the crunching of the metal pole? Dolores couldn't be certain. When she arrived at her brother's side, Jan's eyelids were gummed together with tears and debris and his arms were splayed out to either side of him. His head rested in a fat pool of vomit, already drying in the heat. Dolores continued to examine him: the faint rise and dip of his chest; the imperceptible struggling of his body as it clung to life. She looked, fascinated, at the ruined leg. It trailed out behind him, now another thing entirely; the sinewy brown lines that marked the distinctness of her brother's leg from the world around it, blazoning the simple ownership that is the gift of a border, were lost, and what had been the leg and whatever had belonged to the leg alone dribbled away into the earth. She could no longer tell what was leg and what was dirt. It occurred to her then, something nibbling away at her mind, that Jan had been reclaimed, taken into the earth that he'd so lovingly cultivated—yes, her brother had taken *root*—and then Dolores spun her slow head in a circle, her big eyes sweeping the camp, because something was different, and her impressions and images had been delivered to her in a syntax that was not her own. She closed her eyes and saw a bright pink worm, all the brighter for its pinning against the black eternity of this interior, her own heart—though it had always been unclear to her just what it was that she *owned*—and the worm squirmed and wriggled but hadn't eaten anything yet; and Dolores knew that she'd been right to suspect that something was up, that she wasn't quite thinking with her own head. The air around them was hazy with late-afternoon heat, and nothing moved except for the soft, quavery movement of Jan's barrel chest and the glimmering light on her skin. He belonged to the earth, was halfway in it already, nascent, capax for anything, and she saw him then not as her brother but as a body greening at the edges, a lonely, monstrous plant. If only he would die! And this thought surprised her, too, because Dolores didn't care about things like life and death. She was aware of a presence, coterminous with her own borderless immensity, and wondered if anyone else had noticed it too. How long had he lain there? She dragged herself closer, so close that she was almost lying beside him, and placed her hand on his stomach. The soft thrum of an artery let her know that he was still alive, or maybe only that he had more to give, and then she saw, in her mind's eye, the wet circle of dirt widening, his blood lending the earth a vitality that could prelude life, real life. Jan would sink into the red dirt with the white worms burrowing through it, and from the increasingly shapeless mass of his body new forms would follow; the yellow dome of his skull would crack open and the green seedlings would burst out.

A small, strangled sound came from his throat. Dolores

shook her head. This—would it ever end? Was anything here ever capable of ending? By the window in their mother's office the schoolmaster rubbed at his puffy eyes with his puffy fingers. How long would it take Jan to die, with his leg all mashed up in the ground? Ah, the schoolmaster was smug because he didn't have them, because no legs were better than a leg like that, smug because he couldn't begin to imagine what it was like, this protracted dying, not from the safety of the desk on which he was propped, with his own legs—or their memory—dangling invisibly in the dark air beneath his withered old crotch. He elbowed the Matriarch's computer to one side and scattered a pile of papers to the floor. The sun baked Jan's head into the pancake of his vomit and Dolores was almost as close as she could be. If only he would scream! The whole camp waited for him to scream, to break the terrible sweep of the silence. Who was it that had put the schoolmaster up there? The bitch and her brother were nowhere to be seen. The schoolmaster pushed his nose up against the smeared glass, and the plastic slats of the blinds went *clack clack clack*. Dolores leaned over Jan and he moaned in the stupidity of his pain, and in the schoolmaster's small black eye there was the infinity of the screen. The green trees; the dry earth; the big, empty sky—he swallowed them up from the window, locked up, as he was, inside the whale of the building, and it struck him that perhaps the Matriarch had put him there to keep an eye on things, to keep an eye on Dolores and whatever it was that she was planning on doing to her brother's body—but how did the schoolmaster know that she was planning on doing anything? He knew because there was a *look* about her, something hard and distant that didn't belong to Dolores at all. The schoolmaster blinked his black eyes and waited.

Dolores rested her hand on Jan's flat belly. The sun ate away at her and the worm did too. She was aware of her body, the way it fed out behind her, and something twisted in her groin. Her big red mouth was slack, elastic. There was a drone in the air, which was heavier than it had ever been before, and the sound sank down into her bones. The schoolmaster, shackled to the window, began to chronicle. Dolores skipped her hand down the length of Jan's body and buried her thick fingers into the fleshy mass of his leg, pushing through tangled sinews and bony residue until she could feel the granular dirt beneath him. He made a sound that was something like choking, but not quite, and this excited her for reasons that she'd never be able to put into words, it not being in her, words and their usages, but maybe the worm could have a go, and then its little pink mouth opened and filled her head with speech and light and she *knew*: she was excited because it had been Jan who had dragged her through the camp by the rope of her pale hair, and it had been Jan who'd stuck his fingers (and *worse*, the worm observed with a sorry squeak) all the way up inside her—it had been Jan who'd hurt her the most, and now her hand was inside his leg and he lay slack-jawed beside her, at her slow mercy. Her hand twitched again. He gagged, still unconscious, but there was nothing left inside him to throw up— only a hard white bead of saliva emerged from the corner of his mouth and roped its way to the ground. The schoolmaster covered his face with his little hands, and the trees leaned their heads over the encampment wall for a closer look. The earth was primed to receive. Dolores smiled and pushed.

* * *

Inside the dormitory the children's television flickered on. The sound was heard only by Franta, who lay on one of the grimy mattresses, rubbing his eyes and pretending to cry. He looked across the room at the television. Something wallowed in the screen. The television studio had made a real effort, the greening surface of her skin was caked in foundation and blush, but Marta was dead, obviously and grotesquely so. Her eyes were beginning to dribble and her bloated body filled the frame. The camera recoiled and suddenly Franta could see a shred of the blue sky that Marta was blocking out; behind her, a sun raged mutely. It was Marta's body that hung over the encampment like a great pink sheet, blocking out the wind and the rain and stifling everything in its shadow. Jan's crops? The seedlings took one look at her, sprawled out across the sky like that, and scurried back into their holes. Who'd want to grow up with that smell! Her mouth drooped into a smile. So Jan had been right, in a way, because it *was* Marta's fault that the rains hadn't come and the crops wouldn't grow, but he had been wrong in the sense that this wasn't due to anything like divine anger, but rather due to simple physics because water cannot pass through a solid object, no matter how invisible. And the big tent of Marta's body showed no sign of moving. The rain pelted down on her naked back. What was her grudge? Invisible, she tried to communicate, wrapping them up in the dirty smell of her death. The shot widened. Marta floated in the sky and the encampment lay beneath her, an assembly of toy buildings. She was tethered to the earth by a cord wrapped around one swollen ankle and the cord trailed above the forest and back into the city.

Aquinas watched Marta from a nearby hillside, though Franta knew that the land around them was flat for miles, and the camera rested somewhere behind his shoulder. Her thick, oily shadow spilled over the encampment. Up in the sky, Marta thought about her other body down there in the schoolmaster's arms. She'd like to be dead, really dead. She'd like to be buried in the dirt in the middle of the square or burned in a gigantic fire; anything was better than what had happened to her. Marta tried to move her mouth, to tell the others what she wanted. Her wet eyes rolled back in her skull and a dead bird dropped down from between her loose lips. Of course the dead can't speak.

Aquinas shook his head. This obsession with bodies! Well, when the old principles go, civilization in full retreat, what's left but bodies and their mysteries? But Aquinas wouldn't have wanted to be left to the tender mercies of the schoolmaster either. He looked at Franta and pointed down at Jan's field, which Franta could see was swarming with microscopic firefighters. They carried long wooden ladders and shouted to each other in the language that he spoke with his siblings, their faces hidden by their bright yellow plastic helmets. Now the camera raced away from Aquinas, skimming over the treetops until it reached the field and Marta. She was huge, the size of a small village, and her skin hung down in sheets. The firemen stared up at Marta and despaired. They waved their hoses uselessly. A ladder rested against a tree, going nowhere—it could not be extended far enough to reach the body in the sky. The gray-bearded captain tacked his eyes from one side of the scene to the other. Burning buildings, car crashes, hissing cats stuck in tall trees—no problem! But the removal of an enormous floating corpse from the dead white sky was not an everyday challenge. Marta sagged toward the earth. If they didn't bury her, she would bury them. Somewhere in the silent city she thought that the schoolmaster was still pressing her damp body to his chest. A maggoty tear dropped down from one wet eye and exploded in the field. Franta watched from inside his nest of blankets. Aquinas stood on his hilltop and the camera swung around him to focus on the little white sheep, flicking its tail with impatience. When the captain opened his eyes again it was clear that he had come up with the right idea. His tongue twisted around the first syllables of the sentence, the inevitable line. Aquinas stared out the screen at Franta, and from the encouraging look on his chubby face Franta thought that contrary to all precedent the saint was expecting *him* to do something. The captain began to say the famous words. The corpse revolved in the sky at double speed. Light pulsed across the screen. Franta, still sniffling, had had enough. He leaned forward and switched off the television.

The Excluded
Sublime (ii)

It was all the same to Jakub where Jan had chosen to die, but the idea of Marta left alone in the schoolmaster's fusty quarters was unbearable. When Franta had come blathering about the television and a gigantic floating corpse he had not been interested in his stories about the show but in the ugly fact that their sister's body was still in that improvised fortress; he had overheard the schoolmaster say as much himself, and for once his words had been clear and unambiguous. It was only that he had forgotten about them over the course of the long, strange, jumbled day that had followed his beating and their unexpected triumph over Jan, and afterward his attention had been absorbed by the immediate problem of the encampment. The three adults had disappeared and Jakub wasn't sure if they would come back. They had left so quickly that it was as if they had known all along that it would end in violence: the pole, the leg, the reversal of power. In their absence the children milled around the encampment aimlessly. They ate when they wanted and they slept at odd times. Meanwhile, Jakub lay on the mattress in the room above their mother's office with one hand covering his forehead and his brothers by his side. The two of them spoke together in low voices as he dozed in the Matriarch's bed, seemingly at ease, but Jakub was aware only of the empty space where their mother had been. He understood that he had needed her, and without the reliable old hatred he was nothing, nothing at all, his life up until this point consisting of little else than a prolonged act of petty defiance. Jakub knew now that he was weaker than the Matriarch. Their mother had looked through the black lenses of her cheap sunglasses at the changed sun and committed herself to the future with a body that was obsolete in all ways save one. In the years following the disaster she had been alone, except for a younger brother crazed with the image of what he had lost, but she'd held on. She had dreamed of a city, just like him. It had not been her fault that this dream had terminated in the mud and disorder of the encampment, and neither could she be blamed for the light and the way it had slunk into everything. Once she had dreamed of a city, and it was with this in mind that she'd taken the inexplicable fact of their survival as a sign and pushed herself up against her brother in the hope of starting another world.

Years ago their mother had pinned a map to the wall above her bed, and the children had studied it, observing how the correspondence between the map and the world of their experience weakened with every passing year. Now Jakub glanced up at the peeling paper and thought about his siblings. The image of open fields and black motorways gripped them because this was the image of a subjugated and vassalized nature, thrall to mankind and the stone whip of the city. Though it gripped them they didn't like it. Instead they liked the suburbs that they knew, where the children were often sent in pursuit of supplies. The suburbs reeled the children in because they were things that belonged to the edge. Humbled by the forest, they had forgotten their old purpose. Strašnice, Záběhlice, Spořilov, Kyje. When the children remembered them they knew that there was something beyond their own existence, and this comforted them as they scuttled across the square between the low concrete buildings and the apartment block with the raging sun above it, dragging their shadows behind them like dead birds. Life! This was their mother's prayer. But the younger children knew that there were many kinds of life. They studied the map and memorized the tiny black names, whispering them to each other at night in the broken Czech that they had learned from their dead aunt. Over time this repeating of names became important for itself only, a mumbled hymning against the absolute unknowability of the forest, and the idea that things could be named, mapped, or pinned into being retreated to more distant realms of phantasma. The Matriarch saw it differently; "Only lower natures forget themselves and become something new," she had said to herself as she'd awoken to another white day. Without their mother's drive, how would Jakub manage to keep them moving against the light and the lethargy? The bringing back of Marta's body, Adam had told them, would be politically useful, a way to mark the transition between one state and another. He was the only one of the brothers who seemed untroubled by the change and he had even broken into their mother's computer, though the information that he had found had of course been useless. Nothing but long rambling reflections on the children and their natures; nothing that the three of them hadn't known for years. Looking at Adam as he stood by the open window, Jakub thought that this wasn't true: although he had always known his brother and been known by him in turn, there was an extent to which they had remained opaque to one another despite that terrible closeness, and he wasn't sure why this was but thought it had something to do with simplicity, with the fact that they'd never really had any need for words, nothing to explain and nothing to second-guess. But now Jakub couldn't tell what Adam was thinking. Around them everything was acquiring new depth; what had been clear and comprehensible began to shroud itself in mystery.

In the square below their mother's bedroom, Agathe wailed and clutched her left leg to her chest. She lay in the dirt and simulated Jan: the distribution of her limbs reflected his final agony. She pretended to be Jan in his dying moments. She raged and gnashed her teeth. She pushed her legs down and her arms up and curved herself into a bow. The hands, pressed flat together, resembled a dorsal fin. Adam leaned out the window to watch her and Jakub watched him from his position on the bed. The sun poured in through the open window and suddenly the room was brilliant with light. Dust floated up toward the ceiling, golden as pollen. When Adam turned to look again at him his eyes were bright and dangerous. "It's almost time," he said. "You can't wait much longer." But Jakub could barely keep his eyes open, he had never been so tired, it was as if the others had filled his bones with lead. He let his head roll to one side and when he next opened his eyes Adam was leaning over him and the room was dark. Through the window he could see black clouds—would it finally rain? Adam guided Jakub down the flight of stairs that led to the corridor by their mother's office and then out to the square before the apartment block. Outside his siblings were already assembled. They watched him with neutral expressions and Jakub knew that they had been waiting for some time. Behind the clouds the sun was setting. Light crawled across the square in bands, slow, ineluctable. At the beginning of the dirt path that led to the gate and the forest the wheelbarrow glinted malevolently. Adam led him to it. "I'll take you some of the way in this," he told him, and because Jakub didn't have a choice he clambered into the wheelbarrow. But just as Adam was about to take his position behind its handles Agathe slipped in. "I'll do it," she said, and before anyone could protest they were on the move.

The wheelbarrow clattered along the path between the dormitory and the schoolroom and soon they reached the gate. The dark trees closed in on them, and the wind that swept in from the city washed over Jakub's bruised skin. From behind him he could hear Agathe's labored breathing as she pushed the wheelbarrow along the ruined road, swerving to avoid potholes and the dropped branches of trees. He had never felt the rush of kinship with her that he did with the others, who if they were disappointing could at least be known. Looking over at Agathe in the sunny schoolroom, Jakub had thought of interior courtyards, squares smothered by weeds, a city in retreat. At other times, as they had worked together in the field, or when he had caught her hanging at the margins of their group, too dumb to make an entrance, her distance had disgusted him; he had pitied his sister for her inability to reach them without lifting a finger to help her. He leaned backward, his head hanging behind him, and shut his eyes, but before he could slip away into his thoughts again Agathe was rattling the wheelbarrow. "No—don't go to sleep. I don't want to be by myself. I'll tell you one of the stories—" Jakub twisted his head to look up at her face, gray in the dim light. As he watched she began to speak in their mother's language, and he was astonished to hear not the slow and painful drip of words he associated with Agathe, but the long, fluent sentences he knew from the schoolmaster's books, and these knitted together to form a story that Jakub thought he remembered from another time, impossibly distant.

Agathe said: "The sultan's daughter was the most beautiful woman in the land. Her name was carried away from her by loose-tongued maids and bartered in the narrow streets of her city, where silver merchants and ragged peddlers played on it like an instrument, improvising new themes. Her long black hair became a silken river, her mouth a ruby, her eyes flaming stars, and her restless, slender hands two mourning doves. Her name was Alatiel. After all this the name did not want to come back to her. It sensed greater things. In the cool marble palace that she called home, her sisters watched her with eyes that were knives, and the name surged across vast stretches of desert and stony mountain wastes before bundling itself up into the chests of merchant seamen. A ship creaked across the blue sea. The gulls screamed overhead. The name hid beneath bales of brightly colored fabric and awaited its moment. And when it arrived at its moment the name climbed into the King of Algarve's ear and whispered what it knew. The blood rushed into his head. He could think of nothing else. Yet in the end it was simple; the next year the sultan required assistance and the king gave it. In return he asked the sultan for his daughter Alatiel. The wind whistled through the empty palace. The sultan said nothing. He stared at the king and thought about his daughter. Over the wide expanses of his kingdom there was nothing more coveted than she; the idea of giving her up had never occurred to him, so indissolubly was she connected in his mind with the image of his fortune. He might as well surrender his city. The city, Babylon, swam up in the black space behind his eyes like a great stony fish. He had many daughters and only one city. Still—Alatiel! A curse rang out in the cavern of his mind. The sultan murmured his assent. An ocean away, her sisters readied themselves for the long night ahead. A ball of flame sank to the earth in stages. When the sultan returned home he was uneasy. He loaded a ship with provisions and the riches that would be her dowry and sent his daughter away. The seas were rough, the sky unpredictable. On the fourth day a black cloud blotted out the sun and the ocean grew dark. Strong winds tossed the ship to and fro. The men saved themselves, piling into two kuphars, but the women waited for the gods to decide. Alatiel awoke in a dying ship on a calm sea. Her mouth was filled with salt and sand and her robes were heavy with water. Sunlight dripped through the shattered planks of the upper deck. She could hear the crashing of the surf on the shore and turned her head to one side, cheek flat against the damp silken pillow. Her attendants floated in the water like dead flowers. The ship moaned and sagged. The sultan's daughter pulled herself from her floating bed. When she emerged from the broken hull of the ship the sun was at its pinnacle. Overwhelmed by the light and the remorseless blue sky, Alatiel toppled backward into the sea. Her feet tangled in her robes and she thrashed in the shallow water, dragged down by the weight of her jewels. But somewhere near the border between life and death she has two visions. In the first vision one elegant hand breaks the surface of the water and the young man on the shore sees it and leaps into the sea. When he reaches her, Alatiel is more dead than alive; he carries her limp body to the beach and lays her out on the yellow sand. The young man, whose name is Pericone, decides that she is the most beautiful woman he has ever seen. He sends his men out to the sinking ship to look for other survivors. Her ladies cry as they come back to life; Alatiel vomits salt water and bile. The gods have diverted her ship away from its intended course. Her king waits for her in a white tower. The name thrashes guiltily. Pericone questions her in a language she does not understand and watches her with his pale blue eyes. The vision flows on. Her deflowering in Pericone's bed will be the first of many such violations and she will spend a decade disputed, stolen by one man and then another, moved across other oceans in other ships, subject of a hundred bloody quarrels, a hundred midnight abductions. She will forget her language and learn theirs. The saving of her life is the dismantling of her honor, as if the flailing of her hand above the dark water had been a summons to them all. The name will keep quiet; it won't want anything to do with her.

It will be many years and many husbands until the tides carry the sultan's daughter back home. The second vision goes like this: Her hand does not break the surface of the water and Pericone does not catch sight of it. From his position on the shore he studies the wreck and resolves to loot it. Alatiel surrenders to the weight of her robes and the pull of the undertow and lets herself be swept out to sea, sisters, father, and city ceding to memory; a sadder, shorter story. What did she choose? A hand crested a wave. The sultan's daughter was no dummy—she knew that life, any life, was worth it, and that virtue could be reclaimed. Pericone pulled her from the surf and the light caressed her bright face. She stared out to sea."

By the time Agathe had finished talking, the trees had thinned out and the dilapidated buildings surrounded them. "That's our mother's story," Jakub said, staring up at her, and Agathe nodded. "How did you remember it?" he asked, and his sister looked away. "I remembered it because I liked it," she said. Now Jakub was suspicious. "What did you like about it?" The wheelbarrow creaked from side to side. "The idea of options," Agathe said. She was speaking like them, Jakub and his siblings, mixing their mother's language and the language of the city. "You're getting more sophisticated. You're getting ideas," he said accusingly. She replied without looking at him, "Eventually everybody gets ideas," and Jakub sank back into his wheelbarrow; all of a sudden he couldn't bear to look at her. Ahead of them the road was lifting itself up into a hill, and he could tell that they had reached the edge of Vinohrady. He broke the silence with a parody of their mother's voice—"A ship—I dreamed of a ship"—and then he continued flatly: "You don't have any ideas. You're a rock—a stupid, dead piece of rock pretending to be alive. She always hated you." The wheelbarrow came to a halt. "I won't take you any farther," Agathe said. Jakub didn't bother looking back at her. "I don't need you," he retorted, climbing out of the wheelbarrow. He began to hobble along the road and Agathe watched him disappear in the dimming light. The few rays that made it through the cloud cover were flickering and desperate. Thunder rumbled above, but the sound was distant, rolling in from the mountains.

Jakub limped up the hill toward the schoolmaster's apartment block. The door to the entrance hall had been thrown to one side, and the staircase that led down to the basement was full of broken furniture. He picked his way through the debris, listening out for any sign of life, but inside everything was still and silent. When he reached the schoolmaster's room Marta was buried in the mound up to her waist, her damp arms spread in front of her as though she had tried to climb out of it. The schoolmaster's little lamp had been left by the door, pointed at the high window. The light bounced off the black glass and filled the room with darting shadows. Behind Marta the mound trembled with activity, and Jakub thought that there must be millions of them, whole galaxies of moths, a selfish, blind universe. The schoolmaster had fed them with a slow stream of fabric and in turn they had been his company; he'd deduced from the shuffling of their golden wings and their fourfold lives the promise of a transformation; now as they swarmed over the rotting fabric he was nowhere to be seen. Jakub imagined his older sisters wrenching the schoolmaster from his sheets and felt a stab of pity. The schoolmaster had been wrong after all: the mound had lied to him and like everything else was struggling only for its own survival, leaving nothing for him. There would be no transformation, nothing except a slow breaking-down, and the moths knew it too, were busy with it now, he thought, looking down at his sister's body. The moths crawled through Marta's yellow hair, which swelled and rippled around her head like seaweed around a white rock. He walked over to his sister and dug his hands into her waist and pulled. She fell into his arms more easily than he had expected and he struggled with the sudden weight of her damp body. Jakub heaved. The moths thronged angrily in the place where her body had been. It began to rain, furiously.

Sitting by the high window, Agathe watched Jakub stumble across the schoolmaster's room with Marta slung over his shoulder like a roll of carpet. She put her head in her hands and was surprised to discover that she was crying. Here, at the city's edge, she was overwhelmed by a flood of stolen memories—the flaming sun, the poisoned rain, the shuddering earth. No, no, further back. The university and the theology department, and her mother watching television in a lonely white room. The city was moving, heaving with water. Was this the flood that the schoolmaster had spoken of, that had washed away the old world not once but twice, washing away everything bad and imperfect in order that new life could take hold? Only the chosen were saved. One family had been the start of everything. But Agathe was scared. Marta was dead and the Matriarch was gone. The rain crept into the dark stone catacombs beneath the towering skyscrapers, and the city licked the moisture from the crack that was its mouth and laughed in a way that meant nothing good for any of them. Behind the clouds the moon trembled and protected its edges. It was dangerous to forget about borders, Agathe thought as she followed in Jakub's wake, invisible in the watery twilight, still crying a little, because now that their mother was gone they were really alone, and the lie she had been telling herself—*The men who killed Marta will come and it is because of this that our mother is hiding. She is waiting to see if we can figure it out; she is hedging her bets . . .*—had been carried away by the black waters crashing through her head. Agathe saw the water sweep through the forest and take everything with it, turning the palisade wall of the encampment into a river of wood, while the stone bunkers, humbled by the storm, bunched up together like cattle, and she followed Jakub through the dark forest with the fear washing over her because they all knew that Jan had killed Marta, that there was no other group, that their mother had sent Dolores away to die in the forest. But Marta had died instead, and in some way this had been the Matriarch's punishment for daring to hope otherwise; for her eternal dissatisfaction. Agathe rubbed at her eyes with a wet, slippery fist.

Farther down the path Dolores crawled along the swampy ground, her face held away from the flowing mud by her enormous chest and bobbing in front of her body like the prow of a ship. She was thinking about her family in a stream of borrowed images. Marta was a city, the empty stone city where Jakub went looking for the past, and Jan was a green seedling with a soft plume of leaves emerging from his leathery head. The schoolmaster's obsidian eyes watched her from the window ledge; her mother—an old hawk—flew across a sky that was emptied of everything, a pale and terrible blue. But now everything belonged to everything else: Dolores was part of Jan, and Jan was part of Dolores, and the schoolmaster was too. She was less sure about their mother, but in the great baptismal font of the forest anything felt possible. The moon rushed through a gap in the clouds. She made a beetle's noise and rolled over onto her back. Straining up toward a moon that showed no sign of its former inconstancy, Dolores was swollen with light, a white globe in the mud. It washed away her bruises and smoothed out the lines of her big, lumpy body so that the clumsy heft of her truncated legs acquired a sacred majesty. She turned her head to one side and looked at the water around her. She stuffed her fist in her mouth and began to laugh.

Agathe walked along the muddy path and though the moonlight caught her face it revealed nothing new. She looked at Dolores on the remains of the road before her and saw only the same white trickery as before. But Jakub stood ahead with Marta's body slung across his back and Agathe knew that whatever it was she'd hoped for was lost because the moonlight had caught him. The lying moon had colluded with Dolores, and the loose sticky mass of her sister's body had reeled her brother in. Jakub stared at his sister as if he'd never seen her before. The rain crashed through the trees. Dolores rolled over again and buried her face in the dirt. His eyes crawled down her dimpled buttocks to where the wide thighs terminated in smooth stumps. The human project limped on; life clung to its rock. Now Agathe really was sobbing. The dead world would come round again and all around them there would be the sound of the birds returning, the cracking of the earth as new growth broke through the gray crust—a boundless spring. When she could look at them again Marta was grinning at her from her position on Jakub's back, the purpling head held up by its own power, and the sound of the rain had become a harsh metal rasping. A cloud passed over the moon. The forest shuddered. The moment was lost. Jakub shook his head and looked away from Dolores, who began to push herself along the ground again with a squelching of her apish fists. He adjusted Marta's weight on his shoulders and continued in the direction of the camp. Agathe watched him go, and Dolores disappeared into a thick tangle of weeds, her pale stumps glinting behind her like a fish's tail.

Matriarcha

The sky overhead was cut with alkali: white streaks and tongues of sly orange. Ashes everywhere. The dead soil peered up at the dead sky and said nothing. Waited, perhaps, for the rain to begin again, for a gray slick of water to call its own. The fire burned yellow in a blackened ring at the center of the square and its smoke was swallowed up by the cracked glass mouth of the apartment building. All that was left of Marta's body was a thick black char. But the flames hadn't been strong enough, Adam had said, to burn her properly, and he'd been right. It had taken them a night and a day to reduce her to this, the burnt bones with their shrunken flesh testimony to their parentless ingenuity. When Adam had kicked Marta's head into the heart of the flames the skin on her face had begun to melt at once. Their sister's wet lips were drawn back from the slack curve of her mouth and for a brief moment she had smiled at them again. The others had pointed it out to each other and laughed. But Agathe, remembering Marta's quick forest grin, had shuddered and looked away. Now her sister smoldered beside her and their siblings were strewn across the square; looking at them, it seemed to Agathe that they were as dead as Marta, lying where they had fallen after some great battle with the sun, which was climbing down from its summit and beginning to gloat. Jan had gotten his rain and then some. The field would be drowned, she thought, and the green seedlings, if they'd sprouted up in the bloody hollow where his leg had been before Dolores had crawled over and had her way with him, would have drowned too, because in the end the rain had been too strong and there'd been too much of it. Agathe looked up at the platform outside their mother's office. She had dreamed of Jakub and Marta, and now she replayed the dream like one of their mother's old cassettes. In the dream her siblings were sprawled out together in the sun-drenched yard behind the schoolroom where the wind tossed Marta's blond hair into spirals. Jakub leaned over her and though Agathe could not see his expression she was sure it was bitter. Without warning, he slapped Marta and her head flopped back down on the ground. She laughed, a low mechanical rumbling in which there was pleasure, not pain, and Agathe held her breath. Jakub pushed into his sister and again Agathe thought that she was watching a geometrical confrontation: a triangle exasperated a square; tangent plane to a sphere; Marta's writhing blond head melted to liquid, became an ocean, before coagulating again into an obsidian sphere that reflected Jakub's sadness; the undergrowth surged up on all sides; and meanwhile a saint was hanging himself in an empty town square that was slashed into two distinct realms of light and shadow. Marta thrashed—the dust flew up around them—he slapped her again. Her hair was pasted to her forehead with sweat, and the line it made upset the logic of her bold face; the abbreviated oval flopped in the wind like a paper mask, rising and descending as he thrust into her. Had it always been this way, all time gathered up in that tubal enveloping, the quick, lactic hatred of the heart? A long line of female bodies, echoes of their mother, the same sadness repeated. But the Matriarch had made love to their uncle, and so this coming together of siblings was written into their blood, their sin hereditary. It was as the schoolmaster had insinuated: the first toppling was not delimited in time and the sexual incontinence of their mother was what guided their actions in the present, condemning them to repeat that etiolated moment when the Matriarch had first pushed her flat, young body up against their uncle in the grass. During the burning of their sister, Agathe had crouched down next to Adam so that her mouth was level with his ear and whispered what she'd seen in the forest. He had laughed. "Dolores? He's mad!" Agathe had drawn back. "It was the light. He didn't have a choice." Adam had looked at her without saying anything, but she'd been relieved in some way, as if by telling him she had pinned down what she'd seen in words, hard, dull words that would rob the moon of its power because in words it was ridiculous, the idea that Dolores had been beautiful and Jakub had watched her with that mysterious expression, as if he were seeing her for the first time. It couldn't happen. With Marta dead he would choose another one of their sisters, and although it wouldn't be Agathe she didn't care; it was enough that it wouldn't be Dolores. *Just let him choose Alexandra or Mary,* she thought, *and then I'll wait and wait like a rock for them to die. I'll manage it. Just not Dolores—anyone but Dolores.* Her memory of the night was dashing through her fingers like running water, but that sick, anxious feeling was still there, and so Agathe picked herself up from the ground and ran over to Adam, who was sleeping on his side at the edge of the circle. She leaned over him and imagined Dolores with Jan, how she'd pictured them scuffling in the dust. No, it wouldn't be like that! She reached out her hand and touched her brother's black hair and his eyes opened with a surprise that told her that she was right, because his face was so similar to her own, and she heard Marta's voice in her ears, remembered how Marta had moved underneath Jakub in the clearing, and gave herself over to this dubbing of her sister—her body was not her own body but Marta's, and her voice was too.

On the sixth floor of the apartment block the schoolmaster was stirring. They had forgotten about him, he said to himself, as he hauled his body through the abandoned upper rooms. How terrible it was to be forgotten like this, after everything he had done for those children! After what Dolores had done to her brother the schoolmaster had been frightened. He had swung himself down from the Matriarch's desk and crawled up the stairwell to the upper levels of the building, where he thought he would be able to observe the encampment in peace and wait for the chaos to end. He had imagined them searching for him, calling out for their beloved schoolmaster, and he had imagined their delight when he finally revealed himself. He had waited, content with his vision. But in the end nobody had thought to look for the schoolmaster or to carry him home. The old order was gone in the blink of an eye. If he cared about the world he'd write it into a book, a great dusty chronicle that would be unearthed after the passage of the centuries if a new, inbred race of man were to emerge, swarming like rats across the desolated surface of the globe, breeding, breeding. It came to the schoolmaster then that perhaps it was a question of pulling on a secret lever and the whole thing would spin into action again; a glinting, mechanical movement that would carry them along with it, processing the formless and unrefined until—impossible as it was to imagine—the children had the precise shape and heft of their ancestors; and then they would spring into the old life, too, cobbling it together from that heap of relics they called a city, and one day the schoolmaster would wake up and see them in his sanctuary, smiling, suited psychopaths. They'd put him to work in one of their broken offices! No, the schoolmaster had had quite enough. Now his only thought was to get back to the mound before the smell of Marta disappeared from it entirely, because he had understood that she was the Eve to his Adam, save that their expulsion was not mutual, and although she was gone—he'd seen as much through the bleary glass of the window, seen the burning of the body and her transformation, which was not the transformation he had wanted for her at all, into thick black smoke—he wanted the memory of her, the hard, dry imprint of her body, like a sculpture in negative, to see him through the change. He was ready for the fire and the subsequent cleansing, though it would have been easier with her body tucked up beside him. Thinking of the end, the schoolmaster was not afraid. He couldn't wait to be done with it. Even the image of a book, manacled by heavy chains, meant nothing to him now, though he'd loved them once, books and the promise of knowledge that they embodied; the slick, escapist trick of them. Augustine, Anselm, Aquinas: Wasn't it silly that the names of his heroes all began with an *A*, the very first letter of the alphabet, the story's beginning, and the long syllable of a scream? The schoolmaster couldn't remember his name, but he would have liked for it to begin with the final letter. Zdeněk, perhaps, or even better, Zlatomír. He was tired; he wanted to go to sleep. But it was only a matter of time, he reassured himself, alone again, until the whole damned thing came to an end. He crawled to the window and pressed his face up against the warm glass like a child nuzzling for its mother's breast. Children! There was no end to them. He'd seen her, too, Dolores, the big, resigned body lugging its belly along the earth like a punishment. The history of the camp was a sequence of pregnancies, some more successful than others, but already he thought that Dolores could manage it, that the vague, idiotic smile he'd glimpsed on her face more times than he could count marked her out as belonging to this world, nothing of the old world in her at all, and so the light would protect her and the sun wouldn't burn her and the trees would crane their leafy heads over the top of the partially demolished wall in order to catch a glimpse of whatever it was that would crawl from the sack of her uterus because it would belong to them too. In this way her child would be welcomed into the world. Welcome—nothing had ever welcomed the schoolmaster. Had he always been this fat and contemptible? He studied the ruin of his legs. It was possible that nobody had ever loved him. Try as he might, he couldn't conjure up any memories of the world that had come before theirs, although the others had, at first, assured him that this was a blessing, back when he'd first stumbled upon their trio in the woods. The disaster had saved him, cleaned out his memory. He'd been almost innocent, save for a stuffing of old books, reams and reams of cream-colored paper. But when he'd met her eyes for the first time something had burst with light-bulb brilliance in the black space behind his own, and he'd known it—that he'd known *her* in the city, remembering, somehow, the shape of her pale, disembodied arm as it hung from a window ledge, the rest of her body hidden by interior shadow. How had he recognized it? The fat, stumpy fingers, clutching at life's straws. Yes, he'd known her, the schoolmaster knew that much, and he was from the city too, though already the clunk of their language felt more natural in his mouth than the lilting syllables of his own; what place was there for a language as beautiful as his own in this shipwrecked world? He'd resolved to forget it entirely. No legs and no memories; nothing but the mound and the quiet fluttering of the moths, because the disaster hadn't cared to wipe out the small, creeping things and so the city was an ark full of insects: moths, beetles, flies, termites, and other things that were even closer to the wood, the warp and the heft of it, his old waterlogged cross. A fragment came to him then: "And that was tynt through tree, tree shall it wynne." Something from one of his books, no doubt, the sentences he carried with him. But there was nothing to win back and no one capable of redeeming them. Who had he been, back in the old world? Alone, he'd been just as alone, waiting for them all to leave. He turned his attention back to the window.

The children were outside, the whole snotty lot of them. The schoolmaster cupped his hands around his face, shutting out the lonely drama of the empty room, and concentrated on what he saw in the square below. Adam went first with an armful of blackened bones, and Jakub walked behind him, his head angled toward the earth. The others followed, a long funeral train. From this high up they looked like cats squabbling in the courtyard of some Venetian building, and it was like being God, to be able to see so much and not to be seen in turn! The schoolmaster licked his lips. All those years spent in the city on his own, when he could have taken up rooms here and observed the story of the encampment from the security of this high window. But the mound would never have found him in here. And without the cladding of his loneliness would he have had the strength to accept the mound and perform its bidding? There was no room for doubt, not at this stage. The mound was waiting for him. The schoolmaster would stay to watch, that was all, and then he would be on his way. He opened the window in order to hear them better. Adam stood on the concrete platform before the Matriarch's former office with Marta's bones in his arms and Jakub and Marek by his side. The others gathered around them. The younger children had the glowing faces of disciples because they had been converted by the fire and the rusty metal pole, by the way that these things had translated their siblings into something strange and new. Now they stared at their older brothers and waited for them to speak. The others, Jan's sisters, were more cautious. They remembered the past, the time before the generator and the field, and looked at the soaked earth with doubting eyes. It didn't help that Jakub was speaking as if he wanted to get it over with. He told them that now that their mother was gone they had to follow him because even the dullest of them could see that there was no other option. As a group they were lazy and unreliable; without someone to oversee them they could not be trusted to perform the tasks necessary to keep the encampment running smoothly. Look at this place, he said, half-dead already! Jakub had the Matriarch's computer and access to all that information. He knew about her plans for them before senility had come over her. The land surrounding the encampment was severely depleted. They had emptied the shopping centers, and what little they found elsewhere was spoiled. They had to learn how to apply themselves. Even Jan hadn't pushed them hard enough. The children milled around the dusty square. The older sisters shuffled their heels and looked up at the three brothers reproachfully. Only Franta was smiling, beaming like a torch. Jakub kept on talking. They would wake in the mornings and work in Jan's field. They would make more fields. Groups of them would roam across the ravaged countryside and find stashes of food and equipment that Jan hadn't been bold enough to reach. They would find others, real groups, not the Matriarch's fantasy. And the schoolmaster would return, and the lessons would continue because it was important that they learned how to decipher the secrets of the city and the old world and somewhere in the schoolmaster's books lay the key to everything. The last sentence of his speech was delivered in a voice suddenly weak with promise, and the schoolmaster giggled in his window at the idea that he knew anything, that in his moldy tomes of

Hesiod and Homer they would find the meaning of the last century, the world's causality wriggling through those lines of troubled verse like a green serpent! He giggled because he knew that he had only himself to blame, having failed to teach them anything at all, having preferred all along the mournful, apocalyptic impulses of his own heart over the practical matter of their education. He'd stunned them, bored them into sleep with images lifted from thousand-year-old texts, nothing that they were capable of connecting to the dull reality of the camp and the ruin of the external world. It was all his fault—this absurd naïveté—but that didn't make it any less funny, but more so, because now that he was closer to the mound than ever his weak eyes were opened at last, and he could see that Jakub's belief in some-thing that would help them, save them, or make them good belonged to the magical thinking that was the disease of the camp and the curse of the new world, and in his own special way this was something he'd helped to instill in them by mystifying knowledge, the possibility of real knowledge, to the extent that they would never be able to reach for it or even identify what they were missing. The schoolmaster stuffed his chubby fists into his mouth to drown out the noise of his laughter. Look at Jakub, thinking that the old schoolmaster could help them! In this way he was revenged upon the bitch and her brother. The schoolmaster was so absorbed in the shuffling and milling of power that he al-most screamed when Agathe put her hand on his arm. He turned around and saw the bright oval of her face floating above his left shoulder. Outside the sun was sinking behind the trees, and the fierce orange light that came hooking into the room gave her a hectic flush that made the schoolmaster feel uncomfortable. She craned over him and looked down at her siblings. "Everything is so small from up here," she said, and it wasn't clear if she expected him to answer. But the schoolmaster narrowed his beady eyes anyway. "Why are you up here bothering me when you could be down there with them?" Agathe didn't look at him. Peering up at her from his position on the floor, the schoolmaster could see that she'd grown, as if the accelerated events of the last few weeks had pulled at her too, lengthening her limbs and melting the fat away from her child's face. Even if he had his legs she would be taller than him. He wondered how old she was. They grew quickly here, nothing like his own long childhood, and before long the girls were crippled with children of their own, if they were lucky. Agathe stared at her siblings through the window without speaking. Had he imagined it, that first neutral sentence? The schoolmaster had not been expecting her to reply, not after a pause like that, but eventually she said, chewing on her bottom lip, "I wanted to see what it's like when I'm not there, whether everything is the same or different." The schoolmaster harrumphed. "It's the same. Nobody even cares that you're missing." And it was true—they had always treated her like an idiot, and she didn't even have the blind, naïve stupidity of Dolores to endear her to anyone. She was empty, impenetrable. No breasts! Even now that she'd started to grow, she would stay the same, ugly and unlovable. Then Agathe twitched a sharp elbow into his side as though she knew what he was thinking and the schoolmaster wobbled against the wood. She looked at him with mirth in her black eyes and then continued, flat voice dreamy. "You know what I mean. You live alone in the city. I wish I could kill them. I'll kill him and I'll kill her too." Short, elastic sentences—whipping back. Kill who? How hard it was to decipher their speech, the younger ones—to catch the meaning of what they said demanded much from the listener. And if the riddled quality of their speech mirrored their light-addled brains, then they couldn't be blamed for the way they swam in and out of sense. But it was there, he couldn't pretend it wasn't: an edge of jealousy in her voice, although it had never occurred to the schoolmaster before that Agathe was capable of being upset by anything, that there was anything in her head other than a stream of simple thoughts—hunger, cold, loneliness. Jealousy? It was too human. The schoolmaster was frightened. He said, "What's gotten into you, speaking like that?" and despite the stifling heat of the attic room huddled deeper into his robes, because he was afraid of it—emotion. The dying light poured in through the windows. The encampment was over, *in extremis*. They should pack it up, bulldoze the buildings, and sweep everything into tidy piles; mothball the mine! Then the mound could use them at its leisure. "Look," whispered Agathe, pointing down at the square. He leaned his big head forward, squinting in the light. Something pale squirmed along the dark brown plane of the earth. And of course it was Dolores down there, crawling in the mud, an intensified truth. There was nothing the schoolmaster could do to help Agathe, even though he understood at once, even before Jakub moved away from Adam and toward his younger sister. Agathe leaned so far out the window that he thought she'd fall out of it. He couldn't see her eyes but imagined them burning with orange fire. Jealousy! A glint of the old world, the last stutter of a dying heart. She could hang herself with her jealousy. Down below Jakub grabbed Dolores by one big arm and led her into their mother's office. The other children watched and pointed as they went, and then they began to laugh. And the schoolmaster couldn't help it either: a giggle welled up in his belly, even louder than before, and then he was laughing, really laughing, writhing on the floor like a short, fat snake. Agathe looked down at him and kicked her boot into his ribs, an attack that left him breathless and gasping, and then the schoolmaster closed his eyes and she was gone.

In the office below Jakub was not fucking Dolores but watching the television. On-screen there was nothing but a brown field, above which blazed a Technicolor sky. Dolores lay on the floor beside him, and as Jakub looked down at her nausea rushed through him because he knew that he was as trapped as she was, poor, pregnant Dolores. Life! It couldn't be stopped. Light flickered across the television screen in front of them. Something was beginning to grow in the farmer's pixelated field, though he himself was nowhere to be seen. He had vanished like their mother, their uncle, and the schoolmaster, Jakub observed to himself, and just as inexplicably. He had hoped that after the hiding and the whining and the licking of wounds the schoolmaster would come crawling back. Worse, he thought, sadness overwhelming him, he had counted on it, the schoolmaster's one redeeming virtue being that he was not one of them and in some way belonged to the past and its miracles. But now the idea seemed impossible because of course nobody would tolerate those long, rambling monologues unmandated from above. He knew his siblings. With the disappearance of the three adults they would move further and further away from the past that he prized without quite knowing why, and once the city was drained their circle would widen until eventually there would be no reason to come back to the encampment or the city and nothing left to tie them to the old world, no memory and no history either, only a terrible mutability that was neither progress nor rest. Jakub had not improved the world but merely unhinged it. Dolores made a burbling noise and he looked down at her. "Our mother is probably dead by now," he said, testing it out. She gave no sign that she had heard him. He glanced back at the television screen, but the image had been washed away by the sunlight that swept in through the window. The Matriarch was dead or she would be soon. She wouldn't be able to survive away from the security of the encampment, because although Jakub did not believe in the fiction of another group, the heat was grueling and there was no other source of water for miles. It was still astonishing to him, how quickly she had given it up, but sitting in her office he wondered whether this had been her plan all along—to strand him in her place. She was gone and he was stuck with it forever, the encampment and their expectation.

Dolores crawled across the floor toward the window and pulled herself upright using the leg of their mother's desk. Propped up on her stumps she could just about see out of it, and she folded her arms on the wooden sill, surveying the square in front of her. It was empty except for a few of Jan's chickens, who were taking turns rolling in the dust. Inside the office it was so warm that it was hard to stay awake, and when Dolores finally began to drift she saw Jan in a dirty blue robe, feeding his chickens as the sun rose with love in his stupid little eyes. She couldn't mourn him, not after what he'd done to her and what she'd done to him, but there was a knot in her stomach where she thought his memory was, and neither Dolores nor the little pink worm could do anything about it. A wind wandered gently through the encampment and carried Jan away. The chickens continued to peck at the brown dirt. Dolores opened her eyes again and saw herself among them, a large white chicken with stumpy yellow legs, and felt the ground clumping beneath her talons. The chickens were sad that Jan was gone and now Dolores was sad too. But it wasn't for nothing that they were sad, because it was exactly this sensitivity of feeling that had brought the chickens so far in the ruined world, the whole amiable clan of them, and which had bound them together from the moment their ancestors had clucked awake in the morning following the cataclysm and realized that they were free. Even so, the chickens hated negativity and they hated wallowing. Jan was gone but the earth was healing! All the humans were dead, save for the few who clung on at the edges of cities they had once owned, and at last the world was full of love! These chickens were natural-born preachers. Why not? Their project had been more successful than the Matriarch's, even though it had been hard at the beginning being the only chickens left. It wasn't over yet! Dolores lifted her feathered head to the sky and the others copied her, remembering other disappeared worlds, other dead cities. They knew their history and they knew what was at stake because they had always been made to share in mankind's lot: the expulsion, the flood, the irradiated globe. Now a different world was coming—a world for the animals. The chickens exchanged glances. They thought, as one, *This is the age of chickens!* Dolores was in two places at once. She scratched at the dirt with one clawed foot; she shrugged her large white shoulders and felt something move in her belly. The wind was really blowing now, debris spiraling through the open window toward them, leaves, feathers, small twigs, dust, dirt. The sound made by the wind as it funneled itself through the pathways between the hospital buildings made her think of Jan's howling, and there was the familiar sound of his chiding, too, interspersed with the patter of the rain as it flurried across the camp, full of summer violence, and the shrieking of her siblings as they ran for cover. The room grew dark. The television crackled behind her. She sighed. Jakub sat hunched in their mother's chair with his arms wrapped around his knees. He was too tired to look at the television and so Dolores decided to do it for him. She pushed herself away from the windowsill and turned to face the screen. It was the episode with the field and the little farmer whose crops wouldn't grow, only now the green shoots were poking up through the brown earth, and the field was Jan's field, and the chickens—even the Dolores-chicken!—were preening in the middle of it. The scene was exactly the same as it had been in her head, but Dolores was not afraid. She buried her chin in her plump arms and kept her eyes on the television. Jakub looked over at the screen and began to cry. These days the show had a hallucinatory quality that he didn't recognize from his childhood. The chickens, Marta's body—everything intersected with the world as he knew it, not as it had been. When he had glanced over at the television and seen the green promise of Jan's field, the sickness in his stomach had intensified because Jakub knew that what he was watching was simply an old episode, a relic from the city, and so how was it possible that the field—*Jan's field*—had assumed a place on the screen? In this interlacing of time and possibility he thought he recognized the pernicious influence of his youngest sisters, as though the world that he had hoped to shape according to his ideal of it had all the while been taking its cues from them; a slow, senile, mixed-up reality. Dolores giggled. Had he put the cassette in the video player himself or had the television beamed into life of its own accord? And where were the familiar, comfortable scenarios that he'd grown up with—the abused cheerleader and the epileptic brother? He couldn't understand what Dolores was babbling about, although he could see her mouth moving, the pink, wormy lips clasped around another syllable, blurred with tears and noise, but it was about him, his mother, his sisters; there was no denying it. And perhaps soon he would see the Matriarch in the screen too, imprisoned beneath the glass and given a second life, just like Marta and the others, the televisual dead. The light—the light and the loneliness—had defeated him and it was because of this that everything moved in orchestral sympathy to Jakub and his thoughts; the field, the forest, and the city were metaphors for psychic states and nothing was real because the sphere of the earth was the sphere of his mind. His eyes darted to the photograph of the Matriarch and their uncle that hung crookedly above their mother's desk. The death of his mother was like the blinding of the old king or the shutting-up of his daughter—it wasn't important to see it, but he *could* see it, all of it, beneath the fan of his fingers and the gloss of the field, the Matriarch chugging along the broken tarmac road in her red chair, her head inclined toward the ground. The rain ended just as suddenly as it had begun. Inside the television the white chicken looked up and saw a ring of murderers peeking at her through the green net of leaves. She called out to the others, but it was already too late. A blurry Franta, silver knife in his hand, crept closer to the flock. The age of chickens! It was really the age of worms. Dolores blinked and the sun moved around the earth six times.

Out in the real field Agathe lay next to Adam on the grassy bank and crawled with a quick, murderous anxiety that was desperate for an object. He watched her with narrowed eyes, as if he were trying to decide what to do next, but there was nothing he could do or say that could make it worse, not after the coming together of Jakub and Dolores, who now not only slept together in their mother's office but were frequently to be found by each other's side. The others laughed at them as they made their way through the encampment, Dolores following along in his muddy wake. They couldn't understand it, although they understood abasement, abjection, the mortification of the flesh and the impulse to it—yes, and a few of them even understood the other thing, too, the strange, sick play of desire—and yet it was Dolores that he'd chosen. There couldn't be a poorer representative of their mother's dream, despite her knack for generation. But the siblings were beginning to realize that it was wrong to think that Jakub wanted the same things as their mother. Since bringing back their sister's body he had done almost nothing at all. It was Marek who had taken over the responsibility for the daily running of the camp and Adam who the siblings ran to with their problems. Most of the time Jakub closeted himself away in their mother's office with Dolores, and sometimes Agathe thought she could hear him tapping away on her computer. She imagined him leaning over their mother's desk with Dolores laid out on the floor beneath him and continued to hate them both and Adam continued to watch her. They were sitting at the edge of the field, in which a light scattering of green suggested that in spite of everything Jan's crops had survived the fury of both sun and rain. It was easy to be with Adam, Agathe thought, because he didn't care about the city and what it had been, and she liked the remorseless way he set about doing things, but she was also pained by the fact that their world hadn't turned out the way that she had wanted. Her worst fear had been realized, and now there was nothing to do but sleep through the dead summer months and the crushing weight of the sky. It was hotter than it had ever been before, Jakub had told them one evening soon after the burning of Marta's body. The air was full of invisible particles that trapped the heat in the atmosphere; the rivers were overflowing with poison; and the light . . . Jakub had trailed off. In the past there had been a different kind of light, he had said, summarizing. These days all he could talk about were chemical oceans and the cracking of tectonic plates. At night he dreamed of electric light, manufactured light, the light that they had made for themselves and which remained only as a dull and sporadic glimmering, vanquished by the white, indifferent radiance of the days as they were, secure in their power. Last of all he had told them that somewhere in the far north a kingdom of ice was crashing into the sea and nobody knew when it would stop. Agathe liked the sound of it—*ice*—and the way it hissed on her tongue. Every summer hotter than the summer that came before it. Adam put his hand on her sweaty back and the sensation of his fingers against her skin almost stopped her from thinking about Jakub and Dolores and her fat, lumpy belly. But her brother read her mind and dug his fingers in. Agathe gasped and squirmed away from him. He said patiently, "I'm all you have." She thought that if she didn't reply Adam might hit her, so she lied: "I wasn't thinking about them." "You were," he said, tangling his fingers in her hair. The sun rained down on the field. One day everything would burst into flame: the forest, the river, the city. She'd be incandescent, dead, a planet of her own, spinning through empty space. "I'm thinking about different things," Agathe insisted. Adam looked at her like he didn't believe her at all, but she had already learned how to deflect his attention, and so she pushed herself up again and ran into the field, gesturing for him to follow. Her feet sank into earth made soft with their plowing and she bulldozed over the feathery green shoots without caution or care, and even after what she had learned about herself and her siblings in the weeks following the sending-away of Dolores, the killing of Jan, and the fleeing of the Matriarch, it surprised her to see how callous she could be. Adam followed her slowly, as if he were waiting to see what she would do. She looked at him over her shoulder and he met her eyes with his own, which were the same color as their mother's. Suddenly Agathe saw herself by his side as he drummed out orders from the desk in the Matriarch's former office, both of them older, with their children crawling around her feet, because of course it would be Adam who eventually took over the encampment, once they all figured out that Jakub couldn't manage it, and she felt light and dizzy, overwhelmed by terror. Now she began to run away from Adam in earnest. Somewhere far from them a mechanical noise was purring away without stopping. She wasn't sure when it had started, had already begun to paste it into her memories as though it had been there all along—and who was Agathe to say that it hadn't, her mind being so fragile, so open to contestation?—and so it colonized the past in the same way that it had occupied the present. The drone burrowed into her head and it was this that had given her sentences, walled her in with words. The others couldn't hear it, didn't realize that anything had changed. In the field the sound was agonizing. She dropped onto all fours and began to crawl. Adam was yelling something from the other end of the field but she ignored him. Fire and heat. The trees were black. The earth was scorched. Her eyes were burning up in her head. Who would sit in the Matriarch's office and gaze dreamily at the map on the wall as the years drove on? Adam ran to her side. Agathe wanted to run away but she couldn't—she had been stuck in her body for weeks. She tried anyway and for a second she managed it, pouring like water into the warm dirt beneath her hands, which was soft not just because of their plowing but because the rain had slipped its lid, churning up the gray crust to reveal black, fertile soil, and flowing deeper she followed the lines made by roots and worm trails all the way down to the rocky substratum, where she thought she could see the edges of a room buried deep in the earth, a hot, airless cellar in which their mother was waiting, because after Adam drove the metal pole into Jan's leg the Matriarch hadn't wasted any time, but had gathered up her papers, clothes, and a backpack full of batteries and fled down one of the many tunnels that wormed away from the apartment block. Now the Matriarch was in control of another world, a network of basement rooms that the younger children didn't know existed and her older daughters knew to keep quiet about, filled with supplies scavenged decades ago from the still-rich suburbs, and she could survive here for as long as she wanted. But she was no longer sure what she wanted or what she was waiting for, because the shape of her existence had changed so quickly that it dizzied her. The Matriarch looked around the dim room again as if it could give her an answer, but what she saw was painful. She was surrounded by objects, old, useless objects, with their meanings forgotten and their purposes subtracted away; throwing around the white light of her electric torch, she could just about make out their outlines, which were all that they had left. Where was the elegant system she had ordered her daughters to build? Where were the neat rows of cans, boxes of batteries, and shelves of bottled water? Everything was mixed-up, jumbled together. There was no order. She searched her memories and tried to remember her original plan for the room, but her thoughts slid away from her, emboldened by the surrounding chaos and the sudden revelation of her inutility. Again the Matri-

arch was lost in her head. Her children had cast her away and
even her brother had abandoned her, hurtling down the
dark tunnel that led away from the encampment and into
the forest during one of those confused, distracted inter-
ludes to which the Matriarch had been prone ever since that
first vision had assailed her. She tried to collect herself. The
change had been sooner than she had expected, but it had
not been unexpected, and so the Matriarch was resigned. It
was natural for children to want to kill their parents, she
thought. The Matriarch had despised her own, and so she
didn't need to waste time figuring out what she had done to
make the children hate her, because the answer was simple:
she had given birth to them, and in doing so had made herself
responsible for their pain, because that initial moment of agony was simply the first of many and the following life an
endless suffering without purpose or meaning. The Matriarch had summoned her children into a world without possibility, where the best they could hope for was the momentary
transformation of pain into pleasure as they fucked one of
their siblings, and this, too, was selfish, laced with futurity.
Well, then the world hadn't changed that much after all, the
Matriarch decided. Perhaps once the shiftings and shuntings
of power were over, the Matriarch would climb out of her
burrow and take back her throne. But even as she considered
this the real possibility was spinning in her mind like the
lighthouse from her dream. The Matriarch couldn't stop
thinking about how it would be to walk through the dead
city, to know that some kinds of victory were final. The city!
She'd always hated it. Nothing that followed the disaster had
been as terrible as what preceded it: the lonely, stinging mess

of the world; the heat, the noise, the uproar, the sludgy, poisoned clouds. The history of the world was the history of
God trying to kill it off. Had she been holding out for this? A
great theophany; the final visioning. Or how had the schoolmaster described it? "If only some flood . . . !" Perhaps they'd
never been chosen. Guilt had taken root in her belly. The past
and its losses; her tortured alembics. But the death of the
world had been the death of her sadness, bombed away with
everything else, a blaze of white light. And yet when the Matriarch thought about her daughters, she knew that despite
everything they were different from her and their suffering
was not her suffering, or rather what her suffering had been.
She was not sad but tired. There was a part of her that was
glad it had turned out like this, that finally, *finally*, she'd been
deposed. She had been lonely. Yes, the sadness had gone, but
the sense of being alone, inextricably alone, had never left
her. Her children had each other in all the ways that siblings
were never meant to. She had seen how the thoughts leapt
from one to another, the borders between their minds
murky and unclear. In this new world there was nothing to
suggest their separateness from one another, no real individ-
uation and no real loss, and although in the past this had
scared her, now the Matriarch understood that it was the
source of their strength. If they felt anything it was simply
the frustrated spasming of a self without tools because the
Matriarch had deprived her children of them, though at
present she couldn't remember if she had done so deliberately or not, or if, exhausted by the constant effort of birth,
she had never had the time to equip them in the way that a
mother was meant to. It didn't matter. It was impossible for

them to imagine a life without each other, the family as she had built it. Her project had not been unsuccessful. But how could she explain Jakub, Adam, and even Jan? The Matriarch frowned. There had always been something rotten in men. If she'd had her way she'd have had only daughters, smooth and globular daughters, compact, self-fertilizing daughters with the secret of life buried inside them. She thought about Dolores and saw her crawling through an enormous complex that reminded her of the university she'd attended in the old city, now empty, sinking into the forest. The ruined corridors were full of green, mossy light; gold mantled the broken tiles and crumbling stone walls. Her daughter crawled through the wreckage and laughed, and the Matriarch felt that nothing bad could happen to her here because at last there was no danger. Dolores disappeared and was replaced by the image of her brother kneeling over the body of his dead wife. Later they had walked together through the too-tall grass that swept over another dying town. His golden hair, already thinning; her guilt, unable to be reckoned with; the unbearable agony of dreams—and then in three Paternosters she was herself again. But what she had seen wouldn't let go of her. It would be nice to go to the city one last time, she thought, to see the apartment block where they had lived and the university and to know that the past was truly dead. Had there really once been other people? The Matriarch beamed the weak light of her torch across the room and it landed on the rectangular shape of the rusty metal door. The light. The washing of the world. The marble skin of her daughters. It was unholy; sick. She'd done nothing wrong! The Matriarch stared at the door and her mind rushed down the dark corridor that snaked toward the city, which, she realized with dawning horror, was not so dead after all, but full of a slow, dim life that had no intention of giving up but which was nothing like theirs—the city was changing—the schoolmaster could smell it from his lair. He dug his fingers into his thick black beard. The city was whispering to him, trying to wake the past in his mind, but the schoolmaster wanted none of it. He screwed up his face and resisted the pull of his memory, anchoring himself to the room and the concrete floor littered with discarded feathers and bird droppings, the stiff outer folds of the mound, the close, hot light, and the lingering smell of Marta's body. His elbows were stinging; his hands were raw and bloody. The long crawl from the encampment back to the city had almost finished him off and now he was ready for the mound and the sleep it promised, which he envisioned as a great lacuna positioned between two events of unimaginable import: the schoolmaster's exit from the world as he knew it and the fierce burning that would prelude his return; the cleansing fire, the transformation. The mound and the schoolmaster, dry as kindling, whooshing into flame! And how appropriate, he mused, was the image of a lacuna, which was from the Latin, *lacuna* for *pool* and *lacus* for *lake*, because the schoolmaster liked the idea of submerging himself in a dark lake whose black waters stretched out infinitely in all directions, the flood he'd always dreamed of: yes, this lacuna or lake was its spitting image, the cool, quiet interlude between cataclysmic events in which life would quietly wait for the sign to begin again, but changed, utterly changed. He couldn't let himself forget about the transformative powers of water.

The mound; the imaginary lake. A lake, a ladder! Everything collapsing into everything else, reeling backward into primordial waters. That was what happened, when civilization went. Though it hadn't turned out like that, not entirely, because the world was a heavy band of iron across his chest. Now the others were in his mind again, the Matriarch wheeling through the forest in her electric wheelchair, which struggled and leapt across the shattered tarmac of the path, and their uncle sitting under a tree in the middle of the city with his head in his hands caught in a loop of thought that gathered everything up with it, the same thing playing over and over in his head, the same terrible idea that had belonged to his sister, that they were alone, really alone, and she was the only one who could do anything about it, and every day the same white agony because he was wrong to think that the beauty of the world hadn't weighed on her too, the only difference was that she couldn't let herself believe it was over because it was their fault and they still had a chance to set it right, and so she had hidden herself behind a wall of iron so as not to let her sorrow overwhelm her, yes, she had hidden herself even from him, who had been her only confidant, and he had been too stupid either to fathom what she was doing or to grasp the terrible nature of their responsibility, and so he had given her and the world up, and worse, he had *kept on doing so*, without thinking even for one second about how that felt; instead he had placed all his faith in her wrongness and his silent god, who he saw at last was not there and might never have been, and he understood, too, that he had derelicted his duty and all along she had been right, they would have to fix it themselves, because nobody was coming and indeed nobody would ever come, and though their uncle had thought himself willing to accept this, in fact he never had, he had always been waiting for his savior in the wings, and in his misplaced faith he had betrayed her and left her alone not once but a hundred times over—their uncle could see the idea burrowing into his mind like a great pink worm and now that the worm was in everything, everything looked like the worm, and worst of all had perhaps always been the worm, and so who could say if what he thought he saw burrowing into him had not, to repeat his earlier suspicion, simply been there from the very beginning and he had willed himself to ignore it, and he wailed because the planets and the stars of his memory had no fixed orbit, or rather they had changed their orbits and now their movements were malevolent and deranged, or rather it was that the sun around which they orbited, his guiding principle or fixed belief, *his heart*, had been replaced by hers; over the years she had given him her heart with the worm buried inside it, what he had always described as that "injurious lack of faith," though of course she would define it as faith of the purest kind, faith in *herself*, faith in *him*, and he had betrayed her; yes, sitting in the stone city their uncle could see that he had been mistaken the whole time, and what he had taken as unwaveringly true had all along been the worst of lies; he had been mistaken about something so utterly and fantastically essential, and as he twisted up in agony and wondered how he could go on thinking or breathing or existing because the idea was so painful, so absolutely unconscionable to him that he couldn't stand to think it and every second of every minute was a torment, the worm curled up at the center of his mind and looked their uncle in the eye and said, *If you want to go on living you'll have to convince yourself that I'm not here, at the heart of everything, my truth the only truth, in spite of the fact that you can see me, in spite of the fact that every thought that you've held up to the light and plundered for a sign has been taken over by my light and so resembles me; you'll have to examine those thoughts again and again and again until you can reassure yourself beyond a shadow of a doubt that I'm not here, but you won't succeed because I'm too powerful, even if you do get rid of me it won't last, I'll be back before you know it, maybe even the next day because I've made a burrow and so I'll slip down it even easier than before, and I'll bring other worms along with me; yes, you won't get away from me easily or even with difficulty, let me reiterate that you won't get away from me at all because I'm the biggest worm you've dreamed up yet,* and then their uncle really started to scream because he was alone, really alone, and he had never been anything but alone, the whole past a dream, his wife dead and his sister gone, and nothing but him and her agony—how had he ended up with her agony!—and the empty city, and before he knew it the city was talking about the worm too, and even from the distance of his quarters the schoolmaster could make out its laughter, but the schoolmaster didn't care about their uncle or the past repudiated and now he wasn't even curious to see it, the death of that bitch, because he knew what he had to do, it was time. The schoolmaster stared into the tunnel left behind by Marta's body and could not scry out its end. Then slowly and gingerly he began to haul himself toward the mound and the moths and the slow disintegration of time that they promised with his little eyes squeezed shut.

The sun spun around the earth thirty more times. Inside the television, which was now subordinate to the world, Aquinas stumbled through the long grass with the sheep at his side. He was sweating already and so he paused to wipe his broad face with the back of his hand before launching himself on his way again. The sheep watched the saint crash through the undergrowth like a wounded ox and listened to him think. Although Aquinas was in the forest, he was also locked up in the high tower room where his brothers had imprisoned him, listening for the hem of his sister's robe dragging on the cold stone floor of the corridor outside. His face was pressed against the rough wood of the table, a huge, slumping shipwreck of a man, blind to the beauty of another pink dawn. The name of the castle was lost to him now and it didn't matter anyway because all the words he had hung in the hollow space of His absence, revealing nothing, going nowhere. Albs and copes, his animadversions—everything equal, frayed as the rest of it. Once a producer with dark sunglasses had told him that there was nothing but mutability, that at the center of the universe was a city of doors where everything was connected to everything else and nothing was distinct and the city they knew was merely a shadow of that great city. The show! Aquinas had thrown himself into it with the passionate intensity of the scholar. Now he thought that he couldn't be the last of them, the last real observer, singing the earth's threnody, because his God, their God, wasn't cruel—it had never been written that He was cruel. Was there a lesson to be learned from the dead egg of the world? Aquinas's thoughts sluiced around a high tower where there was no other sound to save him and no sister would ever come. If he had to diagnose the problem, he'd say it was the inability to bring things to an end, although the end had been promised. "A declining, dwindling life"—who was it who had said that? It was impossible for him to remember their names, those writers who had belonged to the old world and who had deduced from its mysteries their images of its future. How did the rest of it go? Aquinas rummaged for it in the junk shop of his mind. "He foresees them roaming the banks of Creation, barely sustaining themselves with the leftovers of life." That wasn't quite it, but it would do. The leftovers of life. No flood, no sweeping-away, nothing but a slow and gradual decline. Thoughts and fragments buzzed at him like wasps, but when Aquinas pictured his memory he saw a gigantic sieve, incapable of preserving the true shape of anything; all that remained to him were rags, scraps of thought—leftovers! The wind slithered through the forest and brought with it the smell of snow. He couldn't see them, but somewhere behind the blanket of trees, mountains loomed. There was something in the quality of the light and the pilgrim's solitude of the forest that made him think of other travelers, and as he trudged beside the sheep he struggled to capture the shape of them, sieving away at his memory. They swam into focus, a noble party dressed in the gemmed clothes and high conical hats that he associated not with his own particular corner of the Middle Ages but with his painted-over memories of it, and the long hair of the women trailed out behind them in the same breeze that ruffled his sweaty curls. They laughed and chattered in a language that had once belonged to him; while there were words that he didn't recognize, the lay of it was the same, the same musical risings and declensions, and a strange, seasick familiarity rose up in his belly. He stepped on a branch and the party of nobles spun around to look at him, and in their identical almond eyes he could see the fear of death. The sun poured through the gaps in the canopy and stippled them with light. Now they wore the faces of the children, pale, anemic, dissatisfied. A story! He grasped for it. A bleat brought him back to the earth and when he opened his eyes—he hadn't even realized that they were closed!—the sheep was peering down at him and he was lying on the ground. "I've got something for you," Aquinas said, beaming. "A story! I remembered it just now." But the sheep hadn't asked for anything. The difference between them, Aquinas thought, was that the sheep simply accepted the sentence of the world, waiting without curiosity for the creator to manifest and for their punishment to end. And in any event it scarcely seemed to feel it as punishment, trundling through the silent forests and forgotten cities of the vanquished globe with an ineffable patience that Aquinas knew he would do well to emulate, only he could never understand how the sheep was so certain that their God would return. It was the same to Aquinas whether the sheep wanted to hear his story or not. "We'll rest," he decided. "We'll sit for a while and I'll tell you my story." He pulled himself up and hobbled over to a nearby tree and sat down beneath it. The sheep followed him dutifully. A bird cried in the distance, something that Aquinas took as a good omen, proof that it wasn't just the two of them—thank God!—and the sheep rested its woolly head on the warm surface of the world as Aquinas began to talk.

"It goes like this: There's an older sister and a younger sister and they live with their mother and father and siblings in a ruined hospital on the edge of a city that was once full of people. The older sister is an idiot, an absolute idiot, she can barely speak their language, and in addition to this she has no legs. The younger sister is also an idiot, though she can speak a little, and unlike the older sister she does have legs, which is at least something. But it doesn't matter that she is superior to the older sister in every possible way because the younger sister is bad, dirty, and sly, and she has epileptic seizures that terrify her siblings and compound their sense that she is not to be trusted, while the older sister's idiocy is interpreted as innocence, and so although the others abuse her and make fun of her as she crawls through the mud on her big arms and beams her idiot smile, it's also the case that they are fond of her in a way that they will never be fond of the younger sister. They don't mind having her around, and sometimes they even welcome her company, and when they do the younger sister fumes because she can't understand why it is that they like her stupid older sister and not her. And this goes on for years and years, the older sister in her greater idiocy just about getting by and the younger sister in her lesser idiocy understanding precisely that she has been excluded but never the reasons behind it. In the ruined hospital there isn't anything to do except work and go to school and sit in the sun waiting for time to pass; there isn't anybody left in the world except these girls and their family, and their mother spends all her time plotting in her office, while their father pretends not to be their father, and so if the younger sister wants to talk at all the only person who will tolerate her company is a fat old schoolmaster who nevertheless makes it clear that he hates her. All this isn't to say that her siblings *never* include her, but only that when they do the younger sister is aware that their affection is brief, provisional, and has a hidden purpose that eludes her; she, too, is a pawn in the game of the family. But the younger sister doesn't blame the other siblings for her suffering, only her idiot older sister, and she watches her as she wobbles across the dusty slope that they call 'the square' every morning as if she hopes to figure out the secret of her mysterious appeal, and meanwhile the hatred in her heart grows. Time moves on, as it always does, and one day something terrible happens, which is that their older brother, who is the clear heir of the family group and handsome and funny into the bargain, inexplicably chooses the idiot older sister as his consort, and by the time he steps in and takes over from their mother and begins to rule the family from her dark office, he and the older sister are inseparable, her slopping along beside him as he completes his daily inspection of the family's holdings or lying next to him in the sunny field where they grow their crops, and though when it first happens the other siblings laugh at them, as the months go by they begin to accept it, tormenting the older sister less and less, and soon enough they treat her as one of their own, as if they've forgotten about her idiocy and the years of relentless torment. But the younger sister stays the same, and she can't stop thinking about her older sister and how jealous she is, and she's so lonely too—her whole life has been so lonely, and interrupted by those terrible, excruciating seizures that no one ever identifies as such; and then eventually she can't stand it any longer and she walks over to the toolshed by the edge of the field and picks up a large metal pole in her vicious little hands and slopes off in the direction of their mother's former office. Inside, her older sister, grotesquely pregnant with their dead brother's child, is sitting on a plush red armchair and watching an episode of *Get Aquinas in Here* with a contented smile pasted across her fat face. The younger sister sneaks around the edge of the room until she is level with the back of her older sister's armchair, and then she begins to approach her with the pole held to one side like a baseball bat. The back of her sister's blond head rises and dips with her breath and the television screen crackles with light. As the younger sister inches toward her older sister, the hatred bubbles up in her heart, and the sadness, too, that endless, agonizing loneliness, and the way that her older sister burbles as she watches television makes everything *so much worse*, and so when she finally makes it to the space directly behind the older sister's chair she's in so much pain that she could be splayed out on a bonfire, and she draws the pole back behind her in order to gather force for the killing blow, and then—"

The sheep interrupted Aquinas with a harsh bleat. "No!" it said authoritatively. "There won't be an ending, but it won't be the same either. I'll tell you how it really goes." And as Aquinas gaped at the sheep from his position under the shady tree, it began to tell its story.

"Leaning against the low wall of the encampment,

Dolores placed one hand on her belly and wept without knowing why. Everything that had poured away from her when she'd pushed her fingers into Jan's leg—what she'd understood as a *loosening*—was being reeled back in, slowly, inexorably, and she was swelling up with sadness. Her stomach was heavy, her body more unwieldy than ever. Franta's voice floated out from an open window, but the sound was too faint for her to make out what he was saying. But she remembered what he'd said as she had lain in bed in the room that she shared with her siblings when Jakub had had enough of her company and her big sow eyes, and it was that her days were numbered because none of their older sisters would help her give birth after what she had done to Jan. When Dolores pictured the baby she saw a lump of stone. If she screwed up her inner eye and squinted a little, she could see that the stone baby looked a lot like Jan, the same meanness written over its small, crumpled features. Outside in the world her imagination made Dolores red with effort. Words had found her, too, just when she'd needed them the least, as if all the lessons she'd dreamed through had simply been roosting in some high corner of her brain and what she had done to Jan had shaken them loose. Now she couldn't get rid of them—a kind of order had limped in. Around her the moonlight came down in sickly yellow spires. The child moved in her belly, and then a new idea struck her—perhaps it would chew its way out just like the little fox in the story the schoolmaster had told them about the Spartan boy, and maybe this was the punch line of Franta's joke; as Dolores dwelled on the image, a chorus of laughter swept out from the dormitory. She couldn't go in any longer, marked as she was by her difference from them, and she thought of how it had been before her mother had sent her away with wet, dripping eyes. Then Dolores heard the noise of the wooden gate to the encampment swinging open and spun her head to the left to catch sight of Agathe creeping along the path to the dormitory, having slipped away from Adam in the woods. In the morning he would join Jakub in their mother's study and the two of them would plot out the future of the encampment. Did it trouble Agathe that she had nothing to do with it, that their mother's long reign had been replaced with a council of boys? She wasn't sure, but what she thought was that there was a sickness in women, whether or not they were swollen up like Dolores. Was it that the weight of the future they carried inside themselves dragged them down toward the earth and prevented them from lifting their eyes heavenward, up to higher things? Or was this another one of the schoolmaster's lessons? She was sure it had been, she could almost hear his shrill voice declaiming it. The heels of her boots dragged along the stone path. Agathe knew that the schoolmaster couldn't be trusted, but when she saw Dolores sitting by the dormitory wall, it was clear what he had meant. Her sister's head hung over her chest, her eyes to the earth. A faint snuffling sound came from her nose as she breathed and she was dirtier than ever. The first thing Agathe felt like doing was kicking the big, drooping body onto its side and stamping on the inflated belly until it burst, but instead she walked over to Dolores and sat down on the slope in front of her. She looked at her sister, who returned her look with an unreadable one of her own. When Agathe reached for the hatred, all she found was a small black stone that she held in her mouth and pushed around with her tongue. She leaned forward and placed her dark head on Dolores's stomach and felt something move. 'It's made of stone,' Dolores said. 'It's a baby made of stone.' During all those years of silence she'd imagined her sister's voice differently: the slopping of water, the rustling of moss. But Dolores spoke clearly, and her voice was smooth and round, nothing like the bright chattering that she associated with her older sisters, or Agathe's own flat stutter. How strange that she'd kept this voice to herself all this time, never speaking a word in her own defense and never asking them to stop. Or was it that the voice was borrowed, like so many of their things? Agathe didn't want to tell Dolores what she was thinking because of the stone in her mouth, but she didn't want to hurt her either. Dolores sighed. A cloud hid the moon. Her words hung in an empty space. The years sprawled out before them. Agathe saw herself with her mother's black sunglasses slipping down her thin nose. She'd have the chair, too, but she wouldn't have to give birth to any of them. That would fall to Dolores, crouching by her side. Their brothers gathered at the margins of her image but the power they had was finite, delimited in time and space. She understood that now, with her ear pressed against Dolores's belly, listening for the dead child inside her. Their mother's dream would not be their dream. Something else was already opening up."

ACKNOWLEDGMENTS

I am grateful above everything else to my agent, John Ash, for his extreme faith in me and for becoming one of my best friends. His insight, support, brilliance, and hard work made this book possible and me a better person. You have been so implacable! Nothing ever seems to stand in your way! I am so fortunate to have you on my side.

I owe profound thanks to Jackson Howard at FSG for his judgment, care, and attention, and then also for taking a chance on something so patently weird; to Ella Chappell for her invaluable work on the earlier versions of the book; to Thomas Colligan for the cover design of the U.S. edition of the book; and to everybody else at FSG who helped make the book happen—I am grateful to have worked with so many amazing people. Thanks are due too to Nathan Connolly, Laura Jones, and Jordan Taylor-Jones at Dead Ink for their support with the U.K. publication, and to Luke Bird for the U.K. cover.

I feel so lucky to have my friends: thanks to Aliya Ram, Maeve Doherty, Emily McCarthy, and Charlie Gilmour, who read the book and gave me sound advice and encouragement, and to Naomi Pallas, Camille Auclair, Ceci June, and Alasdair Saksena, who haven't read it yet but insist that they love it anyway. Thank you also to Daniella Shreir for being such a faithful friend and colleague, and to all the writers at Another Gaze, who have taught me so much.

Thank you to Veronika Flanderová, Václav Kyllar, Tomáš Veselý, Jana Kosová, Eva Křížek, and Indigo for teaching me their language and making me feel welcome. My time in Prague would have been very lonely without you all.

Love and gratitude to my grandparents, Hazel and Patrick Williams, for always taking care of me, and then infinite love to Theo Carnegy-Tan, for his love, bravery, and kindness.

Last but not least, thank you to my three pet rabbits: Pumpkin, Hero, and Mr. Rabbit.